FLIGHT!

Through the windshield Bunny saw the silver glint of water beyond the trees as they sped onto the winding road that followed the river. Jock did not turn into the park at the first entrance. He waited until the police car dropped from sight around a bend, then he swung into the park and cut off his lights, and they jounced down a gravel road in the darkness. Bunny caught another glimpse of the silvery river, and a picnic table faintly outlined under an oak, before Blackie pushed her out of the door. "Wait near the table. We'll be back," he gasped.

As she staggered half-running across the grass, Bunny heard the roar of the car as it turned around and headed back the way they had come.

Silence, sudden and terrifying, closed around her....

WHERE TOMORROW?
was originally published by
Abelard-Schuman.

Critics' Corner:

"The author handles a touchy teen-age problem without being didactic and creates lively situations with believable characters. A good choice for both public and school libraries."
—*School Library Journal*

"Believable story of a high school dropout for junior high and high school readers."
—*A.L.A. Booklist*

"An interesting story which focuses on many of the problems of teen-age girls: parental conflicts, school and peer pressures and the basic restlessness of youth. The Youngs have blended these factors along with a sprinkling of romance into a well written book...."
—*Long Beach* (California)
Independent-Press-Telegram

Also recommended by: A Junior Literary Guild selection.

About the Authors:

BOB AND JAN YOUNG met while both were students at the University of California at Los Angeles, and one of the things that drew them together was their mutual interest in writing. They have been writing as a husband-and-wife team since 1950, and are the authors of more than twenty books for young people, including another *Archway Paperback* edition, *Across the Tracks*. Bob and Jan work six full days a week at their writing, which allows them very little time for their other pursuits—trout fishing (both), painting and sewing (Jan), and sculpting (Bob). Natives of California, they divide their year between homes in Ferndale and Whittier.

WHERE TOMORROW?

———•———

by Bob and Jan Young

AN ARCHWAY PAPERBACK
POCKET BOOKS • NEW YORK

For John and all of The Aupperles

WHERE TOMORROW?

Abelard-Schuman edition published 1967

Archway Paperback edition published September, 1969

5th printing .... September, 1973

L

Published by
POCKET BOOKS, a division of Simon & Schuster, Inc.,
630 Fifth Avenue, New York, N.Y.

Archway Paperback editions are distributed in the U.S.
by Simon & Schuster, Inc., 630 Fifth Avenue, New
York, N.Y. 10020, and in Canada by Simon & Schuster
of Canada, Ltd., Richmond Hill, Ontario, Canada.

Standard Book Number: 671-29535-7.
Library of Congress Catalog Card Number: 67-25283.

Contents

WHERE
TOMORROW?

1

No More Lessons

"No more lessons, no more books,
No more teacher's dirty looks."

Like specks of gay confetti, students streamed down the sunlit steps of South Bolton Senior High School. A tall, long-legged girl in a coral sheath, her blond hair bouncing in rhythm with her matching coral flats, led the pack until she reached the bottom step. Someone called her name, and Bunny Taylor spun around.

Pam Parmenter, towing Eileen Suttle by the wrist, carved a path through the jam. "Hey, Bunny, coming to Frosty's?"

Bunny shook her head. "I have to hurry home."

"But it's the start of vacation!" Pam protested. Behind her, Eileen's lazy nod seconded the invitation. Pam was dark and quick, with tilted harlequin glasses that gave her small face an oddly oriental look. Eileen, placid and unhurried, with misty red hair, was a head taller. In spite of the lack of resemblance, they were inseparable—just as Bunny and her chum Sandy had been inseparable a year ago.

Bunny was aware of a strange feeling of aloneness that had become familiar recently. After Sandy had dropped out of school to get married, Pam and Eileen had tried to be friendly, but she always felt like an intruder. "Really, I have to rush." With a wave, she let herself be swept along by the crowd.

No one else seemed in any hurry. The others dropped behind as she ducked down a shaded side street where interlocking plane trees blotted out the worst of the northern California heat. Bolton was located far enough up the Sacramento River so that coastal breezes seldom reached it. By early June, the temperatures often soared to a hundred. Except for a perspiring man adjusting the water sprinkler on his lawn, the street was deserted.

Bunny's fingers tightened on the straw handbag that held her grades. That was another reason why she had not wanted to join the school talk at Frosty's. She had realized that she was falling down a little this semester, but she had not known how badly. She had expected a poor grade in geometry, for math was her weakest subject, but the D in junior English was another matter.

2

Bunny thought back over nine months that had been a disaster from start to finish. At Christmas, Sandy had left school to get married. A month later, Rod, her one dependable date, had enlisted in the army. Now came these wretched grades! She wasn't certain just when the idea of dropping out of school had come to her. She supposed that, like some murky shadow, it had been hovering in the back of her mind for weeks. She was seventeen. State laws only required one to attend school until sixteen. Already, she had wasted one year of her life. Why waste another by returning to school next September to study a lot of silly subjects that she would never use? Instead, she could go to work this summer. By next June, she would be ahead of her former classmates by a whole year of business experience.

Finding a job wouldn't be difficult. Her mother managed the Mi Lady Lingerie Shop downtown. This Christmas she had hired Bunny to work in the store for two weeks. She could give her a job. One of these days, her mother would be retiring— the Bolton store was just one of a chain of fifteen Mi Lady Shops stretched throughout California— Bunny's mind swirled ahead into a rosy future.

Glaring sunlight signaled the end of the tunnel of trees. Bunny turned up a sunswept boulevard, lined with comfortable two-story apartment buildings. In the middle of the second block she opened the patio gate to the Monterey Arms, little different from its neighbors except for its gray paint and

3

white ironwork balcony. The mailbox was empty. Bunny really had not expected anything. She and Rod had let their correspondence dwindle away after a few letters. She climbed the steps to the front upstairs apartment.

No one was home. Her mother was at work, while her younger brother Doug often stopped after school to visit friends. Bunny dropped her purse in the large bedroom that she shared with her mother, closed the door to Doug's smaller room, which was giving off a distasteful chemistry-set smell, and headed for the kitchen, where she spread a piece of bread with peanut butter. Carrying it into the maple-furnished living room, she threw herself down on the couch and let her mind dissolve into pleasant anticipation.

Of course, her mother would protest, but she really couldn't complain. Mrs. Taylor herself had quit school at sixteen to go to work in a tailor shop. If she had made a success in the business world without completing high school, she could hardly refuse her daughter a chance to do the same.

Once she applied her mind to it, Bunny discovered even more impelling reasons why she should leave school. Her mother, widowed when Doug was only two, had worked hard to support them all these years. It was time someone made things easier for her. Doug, who got mostly A's and B's, was the real brains of the family. With Bunny's help, Mrs. Taylor would be able to lay money

4

aside for his college education. The shame of the poor grades faded as Bunny felt rather noble.

Of course, she would not be able to contribute anything immediately. She already knew from her Christmas experience a job meant extra expenses. Curling up with a pencil and paper, she listed: carfare, dry cleaning, a couple of new black dresses to wear to work.

"Hey, I thought school was over!"

Intent on her figuring, Bunny had not heard her brother's key in the lock. It sometimes seemed that her frail, dark-haired father, whom she could barely remember, had left small imprint on the family. Both she and Doug were blond like their mother. Only Doug, at thirteen, was at the stage where his overgrown feet matched his appetite and his blond hair stood up in a bristling ruff like a cockatoo's.

"I'm not doing homework, stupid. I'm making out a list."

Ignoring her sisterly scorn, Doug vanished down the hall. He returned buttoning a clean shirt. "Pete asked me to dinner. I already phoned Mom. She said it was okay. She said if you'd like to come downtown for dinner to give her a call."

"Now, he tells me!" Bunny wailed.

As her brother escaped through the door, she picked up the telephone. A quiet dinner for two might be just the place to talk to her mother about her plans. She left a message with Midge Willoughby, her mother's assistant. As Bunny tugged a comb through her hair, she studied her reflection. With her blond hair pinned in a more adult style, a dark dress, eyeshadow and powder to hide those faint freckles on her nose, she could easily pass for twenty. She felt a new maturity already.

The pleasant sensation accompanied her to the bus stop. Three years ago when their old car had given out, Mrs. Taylor had not bought another, because the bus stopped right in front of the apartment. Once she was working, Bunny told herself, they might even buy a car again.

It was a ten-minute ride into Bolton. Bunny got off on Eighth Avenue, opposite the long glass windows of Paradine's Department Store, and walked a block down Elm Street to the doorway of Mi Lady Shop. A stocky woman with steel-rimmed glasses and flyway brown hair was waiting on a customer. Bunny liked Midge Willoughby, though somehow she always managed to look a bit dowdy. The second woman, working on some papers at the rear, offered a decided contrast, with her trim figure in its severely tailored black suit and her ash-blond hair done in a flawless knot on the nape of her neck. Alva Taylor was in her forties and looked ten years younger. Only Bunny, Midge and a few friends knew the dieting, dyeing and careful corseting that went into maintaining that competitive youthful look. She glanced up with a loving but absent-minded smile. "Hmmmmh, hello, darling. How were your grades?"

"Not so good," Bunny replied. "I got a D in geometry."

"Oh, dear! And I hoped you could bring that up with a little extra work." The pencil continued moving. Her mother was one of the few people Bunny had ever known who could concentrate on two entirely different things at the same time. "But you had trouble with algebra, too. Math is your hardest subject."

Bunny thought of her disorganized progress through high school. As a freshman she had started out with a college preparatory course. After she had run into trouble with algebra, she had switched to a business course. Only she hadn't liked that either. This year she had gone back to college prep.

"Of course, you passed in everything else," Mrs. Taylor said.

Bunny fidgeted uneasily. "Well, no. I got a D in English, too."

"Bunny, no!" The pencil poised in midair. "What went wrong? You never had grades this bad before."

Bunny had hoped they could talk things over in the quiet of the restaurant. Now, it seemed too late. "It doesn't matter, Mom. I've decided to quit school, anyhow," she blurted.

"You what?" The pencil clattered to the counter. Bunny had her mother's full attention at last.

"Im not getting anywhere in school. I want to quit and go to work," she repeated.

"I've never heard of anything so ridiculous! Surely, you didn't think I'd consent. You only have

7

one year left. You know one can't get anywhere without a high school diploma."

"You did," Bunny pointed out.

"That was thirty years ago. Things were different. There was a depression. My father had been laid off at the shipyards. When a neighbor offered me a job in his tailor shop, I didn't have any choice. We needed the money. You have a choice. I don't want to hear any more about this. Good grades or poor, you're going back to school next September, and that's final!" With an angry snap, Mrs. Taylor closed her sales book and vanished into the back of the shop.

Bunny stared at the switching curtains. An angry ball of resentment welled in her chest. She had suspected her mother might protest, but to turn her down without even listening to her arguments—it wasn't fair!

She pushed through the curtains into the small back room, where her mother was unpacking a carton of stocking boxes. Without being asked, Bunny started helping her. "Remember, I asked you about working this summer? You aren't going to object to that, too?" she inquired in a voice that still trembled with hurt.

Mrs. Taylor's blue-gray eyes met her daughter's. The anger had drained from her face. "No, Bunny, I think a summer job would be a fine thing." Midge was beckoning from the doorway. "We'll talk about it later." With a pat on Bunny's shoulder, she disappeared.

8

Bunny realized that she had chosen a poor time to talk to her mother, when she was busy and tired from a long day's work. Those grades hadn't helped any, either. She had finished stacking the boxes before her mother reappeared, fitting a small black hat over her blond hair. "Midge suggested we run along to Charmaine's and get a table. She'll close up and join us later."

Bunny's heart fell. No one had mentioned that Midge was eating with them or that they were going anywhere as nice as Charmaine's.

Outside, the heat slapped them like an angry hand. They walked the two blocks in silence. In the dusky interior of the restaurant, with its thick rugs, murmur of subdued voices and enormous potted philodendrons, it was cool again, but Bunny felt awkward and childish in her simple schooldress. Her resentment returned. At the very least, her mother could have warned her so that she could have worn the proper clothes.

She was grateful when the waiter finally showed them to a table. She waited until her mother had ordered for all three of them. "About my working this summer. . . ?" she began eagerly.

Mrs. Taylor took a sip of ice water and smiled. "Yes, dear, where did you plan to look first?"

Bunny lowered her own glass with frozen fingers. "Why, I expected to work for you."

Mrs. Taylor looked startled. "Bunny, you must realize I can't give you a job. At Christmas we needed extra help, but we don't have any part-time jobs in the summer."

"You're the manager. You can hire anyone you like," Bunny said.

"I may be the manager, but I work for wages, too. How do you think my employers would act if I increased their payroll just so that my daughter could earn some summer money?" She shook her head. "No, Bunny, I don't have a job for you. It seems to me that if you think you are capable of holding down a job, then you should be capable of finding it, too."

Bunny stared at her in stunned disbelief, but her mother was beckoning to someone across the room. It was Midge. She sank into a chair. "I do declare," she cried in her good-natured voice, "the two of you grow to look more alike every day." Bunny had to struggle to force a polite smile. She decided that besides being dowdy, Midge was also completely undiscerning.

When the waiter had brought their dinners, Midge turned to Bunny's mother. "Just after you left, Mrs. Carter called. She said to tell you she would be around in the morning. She sounds so pleasant, Alva, I just know she's going to fit in."

Bunny, who had started to pick up her fork, laid it down again. "Who is Mrs. Carter?" she asked in a strained voice.

Midge gave her a puzzled smile. "Didn't your mother tell you? Mrs. Brown's husband has been transferred, and she's leaving at the end of the month. Mrs. Carter is the woman your mother is thinking of hiring to take her place."

Bunny had the horrible sensation that the delicate iron legs of the chair were crumbling beneath her. Her mother had lied! There was an opening at the shop. "You told me you didn't have any job for me?" she accused in a voice that quivered on the brink of tears.

"Bunny, there's no reason to get upset," Mrs. Taylor cautioned. "What I said was true. I don't have a job for you. The position Mrs. Carter is filling is not a part-time summer job; it's a permanent position. I have a reputation for hiring saleswomen who stay with me for years. Moreover, it's a job that calls for a mature woman. . . ."

Bunny barely heard that cool, explaining voice. She glanced at the plate of golden shrimp. They would taste like ashes now. Across the room she caught a glimpse of her own face in one of the long-mirrored panels—a young, thin face, vulnerable in its hurt. Those wonderful dreams of this afternoon had vanished. She felt betrayed, and her own mother was the one who had done it.

That was the trouble with adults. They kept telling you all the time to grow up. Then when you tried, they refused to help you.

2

Easy as Pie

"I can't understand her. She's always nagging at me to take more responsibility; then when I want to do something that will prove I'm grown-up, she acts like I was a baby," Bunny complained bitterly.

Seated across the kitchen table, Sandy Mueller nodded understandingly. "Don't tell me about parents. My folks were the same when Jack and I wanted to get married. There's only one way to beat them. Go ahead and prove that you are right. Once Jack and I had eloped and they couldn't do anything, they acted pretty nice." She smiled at Bunny with the pleased authority of one who had met and vanquished the adult world. Her eyes drifted to the narrow window above the sink.

"What do you think would look best—solid green curtains or white with green trim?"

Bunny shrugged and made a circle with her empty lemonade glass on the table top. "All green, I guess."

"I dunno, white would let in more light," Sandy corrected.

Bunny tried to hide her irritation. A year ago the two of them could have sat chatting endlessly. Today Sandy seemed more interested in kitchen curtains than she did in solving problems. Bunny had walked the two miles to Sandy's apartment, hoping to invite Sandy to have lunch with her at the corner lunchstand. Instead, she had already made plans to go shopping with her mother-in-law. "All right, get white then," Bunny said.

Sandy went to the sink. A year ago Bunny had considered her one of the prettiest girls in school. This morning she wore a faded housecoat and, with her dark hair pulled up tightly in enormous curlers, her face had a white, pinched look; but when she turned it was as though she, too, were trying to bridge this new gap between them. "I know how you feel, Bunny. If I hadn't gotten married and had to go back to school, I simply would have died. Some people don't need school."

"That's what I've been trying to tell Mom," Bunny said. "Take Pam. She plans to be a teacher, so naturally she has to finish high school. But Eileen's just wasting her time, like me."

"Eileen's too lazy to put up a struggle," Sandy

14

agreed with a giggle. She sat down again. "You know what you should do, Bunny? You should get married."

Bunny flushed. "I don't want to get married yet. Besides, now that Rod has gone into the army, I don't even have a regular boyfriend."

"Golly, if I had to find a job, I wouldn't know where to start, either." Sandy rested her chin in her hand. For the first time, she seemed to be giving the problem serious thought. "I suppose if I was really desperate, I'd take one of those summer jobs down at Paradine's like Mrs. Valencia, my neighbor, did yesterday."

Bunny set down her glass noisily. "Sandy Mueller, do you mean you've been sitting there a whole hour knowing where I could find work and you haven't even told me?"

Sandy looked contrite. "I'm sorry. It's only part-time work. From the way you were talking, I thought you were looking for something permanent."

"It could be a start," Bunny insisted. As far as Sandy knew, Mrs. Valencia had never worked before in her life but had answered an ad in the *Evening Tribune*. She led the way down the hall to one of the other apartments.

To Bunny's surprise, Mrs. Valencia turned out to be a stout, florid woman over fifty. Like Sandy, she still wore a robe and curlers. "Sure, I think I still have the ad around somewhere," she said, disappearing into the apartment. She returned with a scrap of paper. "See, it says right here . . . 'Women . . . part-time work, sales and vacation relief . . . no experience necessary.'"

Bunny took the paper eagerly. "Maybe they want someone older. It says 'women' . . ." her voice was almost afraid to believe.

"Look, dearie, I'm fifty-seven. When they hire 'em that old, they'll take anyone," Mrs. Valencia insisted with a hearty laugh. "The way I see it, all these young kids just out of school are looking for permanent jobs. It's not so easy to find someone willing to come in for just a day or a week whenever they need extra help. Take me, I'm not interested in any nine-to-five routine. This summer I'd like to earn enough to get this living room fixed up a little—new slipcovers, maybe some drapes. . . ."

After the hour with Sandy, Bunny had heard enough about interior decoration for one day. As quickly as possible, she found out a bit more about the job and thanked Mrs. Valencia for her assistance. "I guess I'd better get down there right away if they've been running that ad for several days," she told Sandy when they were alone in the hall.

"But Mother Mueller isn't coming until one. Even if I can't go to lunch, I could fix us some sandwiches," Sandy protested.

Bunny shook her head. Eyes shining, she hugged her friend. "Sandy, you just saved my life! If I get the job, I'll treat you to lunch at Charmaine's." She flew down the stairs.

It was only a short distance into town, but to

keep her cotton dress from becoming any more wilted, Bunny caught the bus. As small shops gave way to the taller buildings of the business district, excitement bounced in her chest like a tennis ball. At last she saw the block-long plate-glass windows at Paradine's, Bolton's largest department store. On impulse she rode a block beyond the stop, telling herself that the walk back might help quiet that pounding in her chest.

Instead, she was aware of a new, hollow sensation in her stomach. She wished now that she had accepted Sandy's invitation to have a sandwich. It was almost noon. It might be best to have lunch first. She ducked into Suffolk's Drugstore, where she ordered a tuna sandwich, then found to her dismay that she could eat only half of it.

Unable to delay the crucial moment any longer, she walked determinedly up the street and pushed through the swinging doors into the cool carpeted interior of the store. The smartly dressed saleswomen behind the counters looked poised and icily remote. In contrast, Bunny felt all legs and freckles. Even in a sleek, black dress with tons of eye makeup, she had been a fool to think she could ever look like them. Before she could lose her last shred of courage, she took the elevator to the fourth floor.

The receptionist at the desk in the business office looked as unruffled as the single rosebud on her desk. "Do you have an appointment with Mrs. Kearns?" she asked.

"I didn't know it was necessary," Bunny stammered.

The receptionist seemed to take pity on her. Her smile warmed a few degrees. "Wait here. I'll see if she might be able to see you anyhow."

Returning, she nodded to Bunny to follow her down a hall, where another woman was already seated on a padded bench. An elderly birdlike woman behind a counter did not bother to look up, but a younger woman came from an inner office. "What time was your appointment" she asked.

"I don't have an appointment," Bunny explained again.

"It's customary," the secretary replied. "But if you care to wait, Mrs. Kearns may be able to work you in. She's out to lunch right now."

Bunny sank gratefully onto the bench, wondering if all of Paradine's employees spoke in that clipped, precise tone like phonograph records. The other woman smiled over the top of her magazine. "Don't mind letting you cool your heels, do they?" she observed.

Bunny wondered how she could sit there reading so calmly. Even with twenty-twenty vision, she was certain she wouldn't be able to make out a single word. At last, the secretary called the other woman into the office and returned with a questionnaire for Bunny to fill out. Bunny tried to answer the questions honestly. After *Education*,

he hesitated, then wrote, South Bolton High
chool.

At last, she was shown into an inner office. The
woman seated behind the desk was about thirty,
with black hair swept into sculptured ebony wings
above her forehead. Her turquoise shantung sheath
was classic in its simplicity; a huge, hammered
silver medallion was her only jewelry. Bunny
caught an admiring breath. Mrs. Kearns was the
smartest-looking woman she had ever seen.

"Please be seated, Miss Taylor." Her voice was
cool, but a sudden radiant smile put Bunny at
ease. For several minutes they talked about incon-
sequential things while Mrs. Kearns studied the
questionnaire. "Just what year did you graduate
from high school?" she asked.

Bunny's heart skidded. "I didn't. I mean, I
haven't yet."

"We do hire students during the summer, but
mostly college girls." Mrs. Kearns frowned slightly
and made a notation with her pencil. Her smile
returned. "I notice you've had some practical experience. That counts in your favor."

She asked a few more questions. Abruptly, she
reached into a drawer and handed Bunny some
papers. "You might read these over the weekend.
They explain the store policy. As you already may
know, we require a one-day training session of all
prospective sales help. Friday morning you will
meet your training supervisor at the employee's
lunchroom at eight thirty. Naturally, you will not

be paid for this instruction session, but once you are put on our list and assigned to relief work, you will receive the minimum $1.50 an hour." She gave Bunny a nod of dismissal.

Dazed, Bunny rose from her chair, holding the sheaf of papers. She had a job! As easy as that— she had a job!

By the time the elevator dropped her at the ground floor, excitement was breaking over her in delicious waves. She wanted to shout and sing. The sleek saleswomen behind the counters no longer looked so unapproachable. Starting Monday morning, she would be one of them. Everyone made finding a job sound so difficult. Why, there was nothing to it!

Bunny was tempted to rush down to the M Lady Shop and break the good news; then she decided to keep it until tonight for a surprise. Suddenly she was ravenous. Ducking into an ice cream store, she bought a triple-decker cone. She walked down the street, window shopping. She would be able to buy her own clothes now. She wouldn't be selfish, though. Some of her salary she would spend on her mother and Doug.

Doug was the first to get home that afternoon. He had been swimming at the park pool. He bounced through the door, still in his trunks, with his clothes wrapped in a towel. "What's cooking?" he asked.

Bunny grinned. It was his usual greeting. "Nothing's cooking," she replied.

He stopped in surprise, then shook his head. "Boy, is Mom going to be sore! I heard her tell you at breakfast to remember the roast."

Bunny could contain herself no longer. "I didn't start the roast, because we're going out to dinner tonight. My treat. I'm taking you to Luigi's for spaghetti and then to the movie at the Southside afterward."

Doug raised the pale eyebrows. "Sounds okay with me." Whistling, he started down the hall to his room.

Bunny stared after him in consternation. "Aren't you going to ask why I'm treating you?"

He hunched his thin shoulders with exasperating indifference. "Who wants to question good luck? Okay, why are you treating us?"

"Because I got a job today—a job at Paradine's Department Store!" she announced triumphantly.

"Gosh, some folks will hire anybody." With this retort, Doug disappeared down the hall to his room.

Bunny stared after him. Thirteen-year-old brothers! She might have known he would act like it was nothing.

When Mrs. Taylor came home a half hour later, she did not think it was nothing. "Bunny, I'm proud of you. I'm very, very proud," she said.

Bunny felt seven feet tall. She forgot all about that quarrel a few days ago. "To celebrate, I'm taking you and Doug to dinner at Luigi's and to the movies afterward," she insisted enthusiastically.

"Doug and I will be happy to be your guests," Mrs. Taylor said.

"There's just one thing," Bunny nibbled her lip. "I only have fifty cents. I'll have to borrow the money. But I'll pay you back as soon as I get my first paycheck."

Mrs. Taylor looked as though she were about to make some comment, then seemed to think better of it. "I'll be happy to lend you the money," she said, a faint twinkle in her eyes.

She started down the hall to their room, then turned back suddenly to take Bunny in a swift fierce embrace. "Oh, dear baby, don't be too disappointed!" she whispered in a funny, husky voice.

Bunny returned the squeeze, but she thought it a strange thing to say. Anyone could see that this was the happiest moment of her life!

3

Miss Shining Eyes

Bunny arrived at Paradine's Monday morning; a half dozen other trainees were already seated at the tables in the employees' lunchroom. Bunny smiled at Mrs. Valencia, who was talking to another older woman, and sat down next to a brown-haired girl about her own age. "It looks like we're the only young ones," she said. "I'm Bunny Taylor."

"I'm Mary Benson," the girl replied. She was shorter than Bunny, a bit on the plump side, with a pretty, pale face and hair that was slightly frizzy from a new permanent. She tilted her head. "Haven't I seen you somewhere?"

"I go to South Bolton High School," Bunny suggested helpfully.

Mary shook her head. "No, I'm from North-side."

Bunny's face brightened. "Then you're still in school, too?"

Mary's soft mouth puckered. "Not any more. I quit. I never did like school very well."

Bunny smiled sympathetically. "I know what you mean."

Her eyes inspected the big room with its long windows on one side, the rows of attractive turquoise-blue tables and chairs and the battery of coffee, cocoa, candy-bar and food dispensing machines against the wall. She was rather disappointed in the other trainees. Outside of Mary herself and a slim, blond girl with an alert, angular face, most seemed to be married women, many of them middle-aged.

Mrs. Kearns, looking even more attractive today in a black linen suit, spoke briefly. Everything she said had been covered in the pamphlet. Some of the older women looked bored. Mary fussed with her nails. Only Bunny and the blond girl seemed to be listening.

"This is a class. You are here to learn," Mrs. Kearns concluded. "But I promise there will be no tests. The object is simply to familiarize you with your work and help us determine just where you can serve Paradine's best."

Mary gave Bunny a relieved smile. "Thank goodness! If there were tests, I'd flunk for sure."

Mrs. Kearns introduced Miss Callendar, the

tiny, white-haired woman whom Bunny had noticed previously behind the counter. She startled
them all with a strident voice that didn't go at all
with her gentle, grandmotherly appearance.

First, they learned to make out sales slips. Bunny had done this before. She and the blond girl,
Kay Southern, were the only ones to do it perfectly
on their first try.

Later, they received instruction in operating a
cash register. Bunny had done this before, too. At
the Mi Lady Shop, all the clerks made their change
from a single drawer and turned in their sales
books to Bunny's mother at the end of the day. At
Paradine's, each clerk had her own drawer in the
cash register and was responsible for her cash.

Bunny felt sorry for Mary, who was looking
more confused every minute. For some reason, she
felt a perverse twinge of satisfaction when Kay,
who had never used a cash register before, made
an error. "You can see this is one thing they never
taught me in college," she said with a wry face.

Mary looked at Bunny with raised eyebrows.
Bunny read the unspoken message. Kay hadn't
wasted any time letting everyone know she had a
college education.

Bunny found every minute of the training ab-
sorbing. It was difficult to understand the apathy of
the others. At noon, she had planned to eat at the
drugstore, but when she learned that Mary had
brought lunch, she joined her at one of the

turquoise tables. It was fun buying food from the dispensing machines.

"I can't see why you hate school, you're the smartest one in the class," Mary said.

Bunny tried to be modest. "That's because I've had experience before. You'll catch on."

"I suppose so," Mary replied rather unenthusiastically.

Bunny learned that Mary was nineteen, and it had been nearly two years since she had dropped out of high school.

Bunny was startled. "You mean you've never worked before?"

Mary shook her head. "I only want to earn a little extra money for clothes. I don't want a full-time job. I want to get married." Her eyes were frank as they met Bunny's across her paper cup. "The trouble is, I can't meet anyone. I stick around home, then week ends my girl friend and I go bowling or skating. They say that's a pretty good way to meet fellows."

There was something disarming about her candor, but Bunny couldn't help thinking it sounded like a rather dreary existence.

"I don't want to get married. At least, not for a long time yet," Bunny confided in return. "I'd rather have a fancy job, like Mrs. Kearns."

"From the way you showed us all up this morning, I'd say that was where you were heading," a laughing voice interrupted.

Kay Southern stood beside their table. "Mind if I eat with you?" she issued her own invitation.

Mary looked dubious, but Bunny nodded toward a chair.

Kay had bought her lunch at the machines also. She set down a cup of coffee, a doughnut and two cupcakes. "A well-balanced meal," she observed humorously. "About nine hundred calories of starchy disaster."

"With your figure, I wouldn't think you'd have to worry about starches." Mary's voice was envious.

"That's what you think," Kay replied. "I don't have your gorgeous complexion. Starches don't go to my waistline, they pop out on my chin."

Up close, Bunny saw that Kay had a rather poor complexion, though it was artfully concealed by makeup; but the friendly compliment seemed to have won Mary over. Minutes later, Bunny was ashamed of her own earlier resentment. Kay wasn't stuckup at all. She wasn't a pretty girl, but something about her lean grace, friendly gray eyes and confident manner made her attractive. They learned that she had just finished her first year at Bolton Junior College, where she was studying merchandising. Someday, she hoped to be a department store buyer. "So you see, working here this summer is like school for me."

Mary and Bunny exchanged smiles. So there had been an explanation for Kay's acting like such an eager beaver this morning. Bunny realized how wrong it was to jump to conclusions about people. The lunch hour passed swiftly.

The afternoon session was spent in familiarizing them with the store. Divided into small groups so that they would not be too noticeable among the customers, they toured each department. Miss Callendar explained that nothing annoyed a customer more than to ask directions of a salesclerk and find she couldn't answer. When they returned to the lunchroom, she fired questions at them about the location of different items in the store. Only those who volunteered had to answer. Bunny thought it was fun, like a game. Again she and Kay shone.

Mrs. Kearns had returned quietly while they were talking. She explained that except for a final brief interview they had completed the course. Some would be assigned immediately, relieving regular employees who were on vacation; others would be placed on the store's permanent list of relief workers to be called later. "Remember, we haven't been testing you today, merely trying to acquaint you with procedures that will make your first day of work much easier," she concluded.

Kay nudged Bunny. "Don't let her fool you. They pretend all this is unimportant, but ever since we started this morning Miss Callendar has been jotting down notes."

Bunny shivered uneasily. She hoped Kay was wrong. To test one secretly hardly seemed fair. What if she didn't get a job right away? What if they just put her on their list and forgot her?

I've never lost a first-day girl yet." Instead of a handshake, she offered Bunny some of the lotion. As Bunny rubbed her hands, her nervousness slid away.

In the half hour before the store opened, Mrs. Melville showed Bunny the location of most of the stock, introduced her to a Miss Teague, a vague, fluttery woman who was the other hosiery clerk, and gave her the feeling of already being useful by putting her to work arranging a display of beaded slippers. Bunny's first customer was a wispy young girl as uncertain-looking as herself. She wanted stockings to go with a light yellow dress. "Only I don't like pale nylons."

In spite of that brave splash of lipstick, Bunny guessed that she was not more than thirteen. "I don't care much for pale stockings, either," she agreed. She took down a box. "How about this new spice shade? And you probably like seamless. Most younger women do."

As Bunny wrote up her first sales slip, the girl's thank-you was as fervent as her own. Mrs. Melville watched with motherly interest. "You have a nice way with people, Miss Taylor," she commended her. Bunny's self-confidence soared.

Of course, not every customer that morning was equally pleasant. One was a bit cross when Bunny couldn't match a certain shade of gray stockings, and she had to ask Mrs. Melville's help in locating support hose for another; but all in all things went smoothly. Still, she was glad to be relieved for lunch.

In her dream, Bunny had pictured eating daily at some fancy restaurant like Charmaine's. More realistic thoughts quickly told her that even the blue-plate special at Suffolk's Drugstore would make a big dent in her modest wages, so she had brought her lunch. To her delight, both Mary and Kay were taking their break at the same time.

Bunny sat down. "Isn't it exciting? I keep wanting to go off like a firecracker!"

To her horror, Mary's brown eyes swam with tears. "How can you say that? It's awful—just awful! I've already made two mistakes on the cash register, and I know I'm never going to balance tonight. . . ." She pressed her hands to her face.

"Mary, it can't be that bad," Bunny tried to console her. "No one expects you to be perfect at first. Tell your department manager, she'll help—"

"My manager isn't a she, it's a he. And he's my problem," Mary wailed.

"Don't tell me he's fat and forty and pinches you when you lean over the counter?" Kay teased.

Mary looked startled, but Kay's lighthearted teasing helped her get control of herself. "I almost wish he would. At least, that would show he liked me!" she said shakily. "He reminds me of a bulldog that lives down the street from us. Even when I'm not doing anything wrong, he growls under his breath and still scares me to death."

"Don't mention dogs to me," Kay said. "My manager in the Campus Shop is a beast, too!"

It was Bunny's turn to be startled. The comment was so unlike Kay. "I mean it!" Kay continued bitterly. "The woman is a psychological case. I didn't make one mistake, but she was on my back all morning. She fawns over the wealthy customers, acts snobbish with the shabby ones and has a knife out for everyone under her as though she were afraid we were after her job. If I hadn't set my mind on being a buyer, I'd change my college major to something like deep-sea diving!" Having delivered this tirade, she let out a long sigh and her mouth curled in its customary smile. "Now I've got that off my chest, I feel better."

She took a sip of coffee and looked at Bunny. "Mary and I have aired our woes. What kind of grisly brute did you draw for a boss?"

Bunny grinned. "If Mrs. Melville has to be an animal, I guess she's a big anxious, motherly ewe who treats me like I was her first lamb."

Mary and Kay exchanged looks. "Some people have all the luck!" they cried in unison. Then, all three of them were laughing so hard that several older women seated at the next table turned with amused smiles.

Bunny did not need her friends to tell her that she had been lucky getting Mrs. Melville for a superior. The afternoon passed without incident. When the time came to balance up her cash drawer, Mrs. Melville hovered behind her, catching two mistakes almost before she made them. The two of them, along with Miss Teague, were ready to leave before some of the clerks in other departments had finished totaling their sales slips.

Instead of going down to the Mi Lady Shop, where a half-hour wait might get her a ride home in Midge's car, Bunny decided to take the bus. By the time her mother arrived, she had the table set and coffee perking.

Mrs. Taylor looked surprised. "I expected to find you stretched on the couch with your tired feet on a pillow."

"It's her big head. With that balloon on top, her feet never touch the ground," Doug explained.

Bunny scowled. "Just for that I may not buy you any surprise out of my first paycheck," she said acidly.

Fortunately, her mother was more appreciative. As they ate, Bunny tried to recount every single sale. "It's strange, the people I wait on all day seem so ordinary," Mrs. Taylor commented. "Everyone who bought hosiery at Paradine's seems to have stepped straight out of a novel."

Bunny knew she was being teased, but she didn't mind. It had been the most exciting day of her life. "I think I'll call Sandy," she said after dinner. "I tried to get her all week end, but she and Jack must have been away."

"Just wait until you hear my news!" Bunny cried as soon as Sandy picked up the receiver.

"Just wait until you hear mine!" Sandy shouted.

"Oh Bunny, I wanted to tell you when you were here, but I wasn't really sure yet. This morning Mother and I went to the doctor. I'm going to have a baby!"

"Gee, Sandy. That's wonderful!" Bunny stammered. Barely pausing, Sandy gushed on about Jack's, her family's, the entire world's reaction to this astounding news. At last, she seemed to run down. "What did you have to tell me?" she asked.

Bunny couldn't help a small, deflated feeling. "Oh, nothing much, I was just going to say that I got that job," she said.

Later, she called Pam. "Have you heard?" Pam blurted. "Eileen and I bumped into Sandy Mueller coming out of the Southside Medical Building this morning. She's going to have a baby! Did you ever hear anything more exciting?"

Bunny decided not to call Eileen. Pam could relay the news about her job. Suddenly, she felt rather tired, after all. She decided to take a hot bath and soak her aching feet.

That deflated feeling did not last. Her job was too exciting. The remainder of that week passed swiftly.

On Saturday, Bunny received her first pay envelope. By the time she deducted the money she had borrowed, the cost of some new shoes for work, a chemistry set for Doug and a frilly blouse for her mother, she had barely enough left for the next week. She couldn't help feeling jealous of Mary, who was spending every cent of her money on clothes. While she waited in the sportswear department for Mary to pick up some slacks she had ordered earlier, Bunny's eyes strayed longingly to a rose bathing suit displayed on one of the manikins. So many pinks made a blond look washed out, but this was a rich, vibrant color that would bring out the highlights in fair hair. She tore her eyes away reluctantly.

Doug thought the chemistry set was wonderful. Mrs. Taylor exclaimed over the blouse. "But you must be careful, dear, and not waste your money foolishly," she cautioned. With a stab of resentment, Bunny remembered the bathing suit. At least, her mother could give her credit for being unselfish!

The second week of work was easier. When Pam and Eileen dropped into the store one morning, they seemed very impressed with her job. Another day, Sandy came downtown, and Bunny took her to lunch at Charmaine's. They had a wonderful visit, so wonderful that Bunny forgot about the time and was late getting back. It was the first time she had ever seen Mrs. Melville angry. "Miss Taylor, I'm surprised at you. You've cost Miss Teague fifteen minutes out of her lunch hour. When someone works for a living, this is the same as asking her to work overtime without pay."

Later that week, as Bunny ate lunch with Mary and Kay, all were unusually quiet. The two weeks were almost over, and not one of them knew yet if she would be asked to return.

"I can imagine the report the manager of the Campus Shop will turn in. I'll be lucky if they even hire me again for a bargain basement sale," Kay said.

Bunny remembered coming in late from lunch, and she began worrying, too.

At closing time on Saturday, she reported to the personnel office. Bunny didn't see Mrs. Kearns. Miss Callendar took care of her at the counter. "Mrs. Melville says you are a good worker," she said. "The regular saleswoman is returning to hosiery, but one of the clerks in housewares will be on vacation next week. Monday morning you can report to Mrs. Kurtz in the basement."

Bunny felt as though she had been granted a reprieve.

After work she met Mary and Kay. One look at Kay's beaming face told her that she was returning, too. She was going to work at the Campus Shop again.

"I thought the manager didn't like you," Bunny teased.

Kay rolled her eyes. "She doesn't. Maybe she just enjoys beating me."

Their laughter faded and they looked at Mary. She had not been asked to return. "I don't really care. I've got some new clothes, and that was all I wanted." She hugged the dress box in her arms. "Besides, I'll see you again. Miss Callendar said they'd call me back for the next sale."

When they were outside, Mary turned to Bunny.

"I'm going to the skating rink tonight. Maybe you'd like to come along?" she asked.

Bunny turned down the invitation. She watched Mary disappear down the street, still hugging the dress box. She was going to miss her.

Once she was on the bus riding home, her thoughts returned to her own bright future. How easy it had been!

4

The Ogre and
Prince Charming

Outside of the fact that both started with
H, housewares and hosiery had little in common.
Hosiery had been one of the smallest departments
in the store. Housewares, located in the basement
with what seemed acres of tables holding china-
ware and appliances, was the largest. In the two
weeks Bunny would work in the department, she
would only see Mr. Holman, the manager-buyer,
once. The assistant manager, Mrs. Kurtz, a thin
woman of about thirty-five with a teetering pom-
padour of brown hair, flaring nostrils and chill
gray eyes, supervised the activities of the seven
clerks.

"Hmmmm, they send them younger every year,"
was her sole comment when Bunny introduced
herself. She nodded to a tall, raven-haired girl of

about twenty. "Miss Frees, show Miss Taylor the cash drawer she is to use."

Zelda Frees cocked carefully penciled eyebrows at Mrs. Kurtz's departing back. "Don't mind the ogre. She oozes disapproval like a leaky garden hose. But if you look busy and keep out of her way, you'll survive." Her voice was friendly as she showed Bunny her drawer in the cash register the two of them were to share.

Before the morning had passed, Bunny agreed that "ogre" was the perfect description for Mrs. Kurtz. Unlike the hosiery department, where the stockings occupied neatly labeled drawers in a single long cabinet, the housewares extended from the beautifully arranged display tables near the elevators back through appliances and cookware to racks of small items like sink stoppers and corks at the very rear. A half dozen times that morning, Bunny had to dash across the floor to ask Zelda's help in locating some item. Each time, she felt Mrs. Kurtz's eyes following her. When she finally found a moment to rest, with her elbow on the packing counter, Mrs. Kurtz scowled and reminded her of the store policy that a clerk should never appear idle. "It gives a department a lazy look. You might use your time to familiarize yourself with the merchandise, and it won't hurt to take the feather duster with you," she added sarcastically.

"So I spent the rest of the morning flicking a feather duster," Bunny told Kay in a disheartened voice as they ate lunch together. "Even then she

kept watching me. She made me so nervous I felt
like I had thirteen fingers and all of them
thumbs."

"She could be right, though," Kay replied grave-
ly. "Housewares is a large department, maybe you
should use your spare time learning about things. I
do that in the Campus Shop still. I read fashion
magazines, then while I'm straightening dresses on
the racks, I practice describing them in the terms a
commentator would use. It gives me more assur-
ance talking to my customers."

Bunny glanced at her sharply. That was all right
for Kay, who was planning a fashion career, but
she had no desire to spend the rest of her life in
housewares. She suddenly missed Mary, who
would have been more sympathetic.

After lunch things went a little better. In her
spare moments, Bunny seized the duster and kept
as many aisles as possible between herself and
Mrs. Kurtz. It was only at the end of the day when
she added up her sales slips and counted the
money in her drawer that her heart sank. She was
$3.15 off. In desperation, she glanced around to
see if Zelda was near. It was too late. Mrs. Kurtz
was already bearing down on her.

"I can't seem to balance," Bunny faltered.

"Well, go over your figures again," Mrs. Kurtz
advised.

"I have—three times," Bunny protested. "I
thought . . . if you could help me?"

Mrs. Kurtz's face froze. "Miss Taylor, I have

eight cash drawers to check. I can't play nursemaid to every employee who makes an error. In this department we correct our own mistakes."

Bunny blushed as she saw the amused eyes of other clerks. A miserable, choking feeling in her throat, she went over the figures again. Mrs. Kurtz raised questioning eyebrows. Bunny shook her head. On the next try, she found it, such a simple error in addition that it seemed unbelievable.

Mrs. Kurtz did not bother to check her sales book. "I'm glad you found it, Miss Taylor. Remember, there are two things I will not tolerate in this department: carelessness and leaning on others." She paused, and her cold gray eyes seemed to bore into Bunny's. "And I might add, when I see someone who spends an afternoon trying to avoid me purposely, I'm bound to be suspicious."

She strode away, leaving Bunny feeling as though she had been slapped in the face.

Paradine's was open Monday nights. Over the week end, Bunny had planned how she would spend her second paycheck: a new, tailored dress for work, a couple of slips and the rest to start a savings account. After such a miserable day, the thought of underwear and shirtwaist frocks did little to lift her spirits. On impulse, she rode the elevator to the third floor and sportswear. The rose bathing suit was still on the manikin! It cost twenty-five dollars, twice what she usually paid for a bathing suit, but the moment she tried it on she knew it was for her. It performed flattering miracles for her slim figure and made her look at least two years older. Most of all, it had a kind of magic quality that seemed to promise that a girl who owned a suit like that would have all kinds of adventures.

By the time she added a terrycloth cape and beach bag, a pair of rope-soled sandals and a crazy straw hat with a bouncing fringe, the bill came to forty dollars. As she rode home on the bus, clutching her packages, the unpleasant day faded into insignificance. All she had to do was to get through tomorrow. Wednesday was the Fourth of July. Then Thursday was her regular day off. Two weeks would pass quickly, and she would be transferred to some other department.

"Forty dollars for a swimming outfit. Isn't that extravagant?" Mrs. Taylor exclaimed.

"It's my money," Bunny said.

"Yes, it's your money," her mother agreed, "but where do you expect to wear it? You hardly ever go swimming."

Bunny realized unhappily that this was true. After all she had suffered that day, it was hard to accept any more criticism. "I'll wear it on the Fourth and go to the park pool!"

Somehow, she survived the following day without aggravating Mrs. Kurtz. It was very pleasant to sleep late on the morning of the Fourth. Later, when she phoned Pam and Eileen, she found to her disappointment that they were spending the holiday out of town. Even Doug had been invited on a picnic. At one o'clock, with the new suit tucked into her beach bag, she started for the park alone.

The day was hot. Before she had gone a block, little rivulets of perspiration were trickling between her shoulder blades. At the park, the playground was a mass of shrieking children, and every picnic table was taken. The pool was crowded too. Except for a small blue-green opening beneath the diving board, the water was speckled with bobbing heads. Once she had changed into the rose suit, Bunny decided against going in right away. She found a spot next to the fence, where she sprawled on her beach towel.

Not all the sunbathers were fortunate enough to find places out of the way of the crowd. Bunny had barely made herself comfortable when a tall boy with crew-cut red hair spread his towel on the deck a few feet away. Before he lay down, his eyes swept toward her in a look that was frankly admiring.

He couldn't have chosen a worse spot. Three boys chasing each other had to jump over him, the last one kicking him in the shoulder. An arguing couple backed up, and one of them trod on his hand. With a disgusted sigh, he rose.

His eyes met Bunny's. "Look, I'm not trying to be fresh or anything, but if I keep laying out here I'm going to be a squashed plum. Mind if I crowd in next to you?" he asked.

Bunny shook her head and edged over so there was room next to the fence. He spread his towel and plopped down heavily. Lying side by side with someone, so close that your elbows touched, it was hard not to be friendly. Their eyes met, and they exchanged smiles again.

He rolled over suddenly and leaned on one elbow. "Look, I'm an awful liar," he said. "I never intended to lie out there and let that mob trample me. I spotted you the moment you came in. I wanted to meet you, but you didn't look like the kind of a girl who lets a fellow pick her up. Letting those dirty little urchins kick me in the head was just a ruse to get your sympathy."

His frankness caught Bunny off guard, but she was flattered. He looked older than any of the boys she knew, but he had a disarming smile. Instead of the usual freckles that went with red hair, he was deeply tanned, with the lean, muscular look of an athlete. "You're right, I'm not that kind of girl," she agreed, then wrinkled her nose. "But I'm very tender-hearted."

He chuckled and gave a satisfied nod. "In that case, let's get on with introductions. I'm Dan Harding: kind to my mother, adored by my cocker spaniel and hoping to be high scorer on the Bolton JC basketball team next year—in case you're the kind of girl who expects her dates to be big men on campus."

"No, I'm not that kind of girl, either," Bunny

protested. "I have a friend who goes to JC—Kay Southern. Maybe you know her?"

Dan shook his head. "No, though the name sounds familiar. But I'm sure if you tell me all about yourself we'll find some mutual acquaintance." When he was laughing, his gray eyes had gold flecks in them.

Bunny hesitated. He was in his second year of college. If he knew she was only in high school, he might lose interest. "My name's Bunny Taylor, and I work at Paradine's," she said.

Dan quirked an eyebrow. "A woman of the world, eh? I bought a necktie there once—blue with gray stripes. That should be enough to make us old buddies."

Bunny laughed. He was different from anyone she had met before. Suddenly, she was different, too. Instead of being tongue-tied, she found herself tossing back Dan's banter as easily as though she had done it for years.

Later, they took a dip in the pool, then returned to their towels and sunbathed again. All too soon, Bunny saw that the clock above the lifeguard's stand said four o'clock. Dan must have guessed what was going through her mind.

"Meet me outside. We'll go somewhere for something to eat, then I'll drive you home."

Bunny started to accept, then stopped as she remembered her mother's warnings about accepting rides with strangers. Dan seemed nice, but she had never seen him before this afternoon. She had no way of knowing that any of the things he had told her were true. What would her mother say if she saw her riding home with a total stranger? But if she told him the truth, he might think she was awfully young.

"I'd love to, really, but I'm already meeting someone who is driving me home," she lied.

He was silent, and Bunny's heart sank. She would never see him again. Then abruptly he grinned. "How about giving me your phone number, then? I'll call you later; maybe we can do something tomorrow?"

Bunny felt as though a huge knot had loosened in her chest. As they stood up, Dan made a helpless motion toward his trunks. It was obvious that he had no way to write down her number. "But I have a good memory. I'll remember it until I get to my locker," he promised. He repeated the number three times before they said good-bye.

Bunny took her time dressing so that she would not run into Dan outside. She was glad she had bought the bathing suit now. Already exciting things were beginning to happen to her.

When Bunny reached home, she saw that her mother had changed into a fresh cotton dress. She explained that after dinner Midge had offered to drive them to the park to see the fireworks. "You'll come too, won't you?" she asked.

Bunny felt a little catch in her throat. "If you

don't mind, I think I'll stay home. I'm kind of tired."

When her mother and Midge had gone, she wandered restlessly about the apartment, waiting for Dan to call. Outside, it slowly grew dark. Far to the south the first of the fireworks sprayed like a golden chrysanthemum above the trees of the park. If Dan asked her out tomorrow, Bunny wondered how she would explain him to her mother.

But she had worried for nothing. There was no telephone call.

Friday morning Bunny and Kay were having a cup of coffee before the store opened when Zelda joined them. The conversation turned to the holiday. "You mean after spending the whole afternoon with him, you still were afraid to let him drive you home?" Zelda gasped incredulously when she heard about Dan.

Bunny scowled into her coffee cup and wished Zelda didn't have that infuriating way of making her feel about ten years old. "My mother doesn't let me accept rides with strangers," she explained.

"What does your mother have to do with it?" Zelda teased.

"Well, I live at home," Bunny said lamely.

"So do I!" Zelda replied. "But if I'm able to earn my own living, I figure I have a right to choose my own friends."

Kay must have seen the hurt in Bunny's eyes. "Remember, Bunny's only seventeen. I think she did the right thing," she said. She patted Bunny's shoulder reassuringly. "But if it will make you feel any better, Dan Harding really does go to Bolton JC. I don't know him personally, but he plays on the basketball team."

Bunny knew Kay meant to be comforting, but somehow the knowledge that Dan had not been lying only made her feel worse. Zelda was right. She had acted like an infant. As a result, she'd lost out on a date with the most interesting boy she'd ever met.

Later, Bunny told herself it was the upset about Zelda's teasing that caused her to make such an awful mistake that morning. It was one of her larger sales: a brass sunburst clock that cost almost fifty dollars. Apparently, the woman had decided on the clock previously, for she made the selection quickly and seemed to be in a hurry. She had almost reached the elevator when Bunny realized she had forgotten to add the sales tax.

For a moment, she stood paralyzed. If she ran, there was still a chance to catch the woman, but that would attract everyone's attention. While she hesitated, the customer vanished into the elevator.

Bunny closed her sales book with trembling fingers. She would pretend the error had never happened. Her cash would still balance tonight, and Mrs. Kurtz seldom checked sales books.

As though guided by radar, Mrs. Kurtz came down the center aisle. "That was a nice sale. I hope you remembered your tax."

Bunny drew a painful breath. Having made one wrong decision, it was surprisingly easy to make another. "Oh, yes," she lied.

Her breath escaped in a grateful sigh as the assistant manager continued down the aisle. Picking up the feather duster, she made herself very busy.

At ten-thirty, she was released for her morning break. Normally, Bunny took advantage of the brief rest periods to sprawl on one of the couches in the employee's lounge. Today, she was too restless to sit down. She returned to the floor several minutes early. Mrs. Kurtz stood by the cash register. "Miss Taylor, I want to speak to you." Reaching under the counter, she brought out Bunny's sales book. "Why did you lie to me?"

If there had been a second basement, Bunny's heart would have plummeted into it. "I don't know...," she stammered.

Mrs. Kurtz flipped open the book. "I mean the sale of that sunburst clock. I distinctly asked you if you had charged tax. You just as distinctly told me you had. Now, I ask you, why did you lie?"

Bunny realized miserably that there was nothing to do but to tell the truth. "I didn't want you to know I had made a mistake. I thought it wouldn't matter."

"You thought it wouldn't matter?" Mrs. Kurtz gasped. Her voice rose so loudly that customers and clerks turned to stare. "Miss Taylor, you're in the business world now, not a classroom. Here, someone doesn't hand you back your paper at the end of the day with your mistakes corrected and the fond hope that you will learn next time. Here, you are supposed to have learned already. If you make a mistake, you correct it immediately. How many employees do you think Paradine's has?"

Bunny looked confused. "Over a hundred?"

Mrs. Kurtz nodded. "And just what do you think would happen if every one of those employees made a two-dollar error today and tried to cover it up? Have you any idea of how much that would cost the store, plus the confusion it would cause the bookkeepers?"

Bunny felt even more miserable than before. "I'll pay the money out of my own purse," she offered.

"That won't be necessary this time," Mrs. Kurtz snapped, "but if it happens again, you will have to make it up. Just see that there is no more lying. Your purpose in this department is to sell housewares, not to figure out methods to get around me!"

Bunny realized that everyone in the department had witnessed the scene. Only pride held back the tears. Thankful that she did not have to wait on any customers right then, she busied herself unpacking some dishrags.

When Mrs. Kurtz had gone, Zelda brushed against her. "The old hag. So you made a mistake.

She didn't have to bawl you out in front of everyone."

"No matter how I try, I'll never please her," Bunny said despondently.

"Look, maybe we can help each other," Zelda suggested.

Bunny's forehead knotted. "How?"

"Well, you're a relief worker, so you get paid by the hour, but I'm a regular saleswoman, so I work on commission, too. It doesn't matter how many sales you make, but I have a weekly quota, and above that I get an extra bonus." Zelda eyed Bunny shrewdly. "Now if you let me write up some of your sales slips, it would help me and—"

"I won't make so many mistakes or have so many slips to add up at the end of the day!" Bunny interrupted enthusiastically. It sounded like a fine idea.

The next day and the first of the following week, it seemed to Bunny that things went more smoothly in housewares. She still waited on customers, but whenever she and Zelda turned up at the cash register at the same time, she let Zelda write both sales slips while she boxed and wrapped the purchases. When there was a choice of putting away stock or waiting on customers, she chose the former.

Wednesday afternoon, she was balanced on a ladder putting away a toaster when she heard a flattering whistle behind her. She swung around angrily. Leaning one elbow on the counter, chin in

his hand and gray eyes twinkling, was Dan
Harding.

"Why . . . hi," she stammered.

"Hi!" he repeated scornfully. "All she can say is
'Hi' when I have been scouring every street, wearing my soles thin just searching for her."

There was something about his light banter that
enveloped Bunny so that they were right back
there beside the pool again, and the week since
they had said good-bye had never existed.

"Your shoes don't look very worn to me," she
said tartly, climbing down from the ladder.

"Don't let appearances deceive you; this is my
second pair," Dan replied. "I didn't have a pencil
in my locker, so of course I forgot your telephone
number. Do you know how many Taylors there are
in the phone book? That left only Paradine's. I was
pretty sure you were a salesgirl. Only I didn't know
the department. Do you know how long it has
taken me to cover every inch of this store, ogling
at salesgirls? It wasn't so bad on the first floor, but
up on the third, where it's all ladies' wear, fat
women screamed, girls tittered and I got so red
someone turned in a fire alarm. But here I am—"
He held out his palms expressively.

The thought dashed through Bunny's mind that
if he had been so anxious he wouldn't have waited
a whole week, but there was no resisting that
teasing smile. "Here you are," she repeated.
Suddenly, even here in the blue artificial light of
the basement, the sun was shining. He hadn't

forgotten her like Zelda had hinted. He had gone to all this effort to find her.

"Young woman, if it wouldn't be too much trouble, could you wait on me?" a customer's angry voice cut through their laughter.

Bunny spun around guiltily.

"When do you get off work? I'll drive you home," Dan said.

"In forty minutes, the Elm Street entrance," Bunny replied. Hurriedly, she waved when he reached the elevator. "I'm terribly sorry," she apologized to the customer.

The customer responded with a sniff. Bunny tried to smile pleasantly. She hoped that she would never get so old that she couldn't wait for a girl to say good-bye to her boyfriend!

She had never known forty minutes to go so slowly. Finally, they were over. Dan was waiting at the Elm Street door. They walked to his car, a conservative green coupe that was neither young nor old. Bunny didn't protest about his driving her home this time.

"This way I'll know where to pick you up tonight when we go to the show," he said as he threaded his way through the evening traffic.

Bunny glanced at him sharply. He seemed very sure of himself. Then she grinned. Why was she complaining? Just wait until Pam and Eileen heard she was dating a college man!

"Just where did you say you met this Dan

Harding?" Bunny's mother questioned her as they were eating dinner.

Bunny dropped her eyes to her plate. She hadn't said. "He stopped by the store today. You remember my telling you about Kay Southern? They both go to Bolton JC." She assured herself that she hadn't told an outright lie. She hadn't actually said that Kay had introduced them.

Her mother's forehead puckered, but she said nothing. Bunny worried that her mother might not approve of Dan with his brash ways and teasing laughter, but when he called at eight he wore a conservative dark suit and was very polite and she could see that her mother liked him right away. With an odd jolt she realized that she probably could have told her the truth from the beginning!

They had a wonderful evening. Dan held her hand in the show and driving home he draped his arm along the back of the seat but he didn't try to get fresh, and he invited her out again on Saturday. The next morning she went to work at Paradine's with a feeling she was walking on clouds.

The feeling didn't last. She had barely started making up her cash drawer when Mrs. Kurtz stopped beside her. "Was it your idea or Zelda Frees's that she write up some of your sales?"

Bunny stiffened. "As long as we both work hard, I can't see where it hurts anyone. She's more accurate, and I don't work on a commission."

"Experience is what teaches one to be accurate," Mrs. Kurtz reminded her. "As for not hurting anyone, Personnel watches you relief workers, too. They have an idea of about how many sales a good worker should write in one day. Every time you let Miss Frees rob you of a sale, you're hurting your own chances of being hired again."

Bunny was aware of a wretched sinking feeling. She wondered what she was going to say to Zelda. She did not have to say anything. Mrs. Kurtz must have reached her first. Five minutes later, Zelda came down the aisle, her black eyes flashing. "Thanks a lot, you little snitch!" she said savagely.

Bunny did not bother to protest that Mrs. Kurtz had guessed the truth. For her remaining days in housewares, she added Zelda to her list of people to be avoided.

Kay had already learned that she was being kept on in the Campus Shop for the remainder of the summer. Saturday night, as Bunny went upstairs to pick up her check, she had the sick, cold feeling that she would not be asked to return. Her work in housewares had hardly been outstanding.

"I'm afraid we don't have any openings in sales work this next week." Miss Callendar confirmed her worst fears. Then she gave Bunny a friendly smile. "But one of our stock girls in the wrapping department quit unexpectedly this week. It's simple work and might develop into a job for the rest of the summer."

Bunny left the store, walking on that cloud again. Maybe being a wrapping clerk wasn't as romantic as sales work, but she still had a job. She was dating Dan. For all her ups and downs these last weeks, her life had never been this exciting before!

5

Dropout!

The blue denim smocks worn by the women of the wrapping and mailing department managed to make even the trimmest figure look dumpily middle-aged, but since their only contact with the public was through the gift-wrapping counter, Bunny supposed high fashion was unimportant.

Miss Holly, her immediate superior, was a happy medium betwen solicitous Mrs. Melville and rigid, demanding Mrs. Kurtz. Cheri Mays, a tall, unruffled blond who continually chewed gum, was Bunny's working partner. Slightly above them in rank was Mrs. Ashford, an older clerk, who handled the gift-wrapping counter.

Most of Paradine's orders were sent by truck from the shipping department, but enough customers requested mail delivery to keep Cheri and

Bunny busy. A door at one end of the mail room opened directly into the box- and ribbon-lined cubicle behind the gift-wrapping counter. This was the special domain of Mrs. Ashford, but during the day if the customers got ahead of her or if she wished to take a break, she would ring a small bell. One of the girls would leave her work and step into the cubicle to help.

The other break in the monotonous routine came only once a day but was far more exciting. The prima donna of Paradine's was Miss Inez DeWitt, a statuesque brunette with a voice like warm honey, who appeared in a weekly television program and directed the store's personal shopping service. Most of her work was done from her office on the fourth floor, but once each morning she made a grand tour of the store to personally select some of the more difficult items. Since these usually had to be gift-wrapped, one of the clerks from the mailing department usually went with her. The first time Bunny was assigned to Miss DeWitt, she trailed her from department to department in a haze of admiration.

"Imagine a job like that—being paid to go shopping!" she told Kay enthusiastically at lunch.

Kay laughed. "It sounds good, doesn't it? Only imagine how it feels to buy all those lovely things and never get to keep any of them."

"I hadn't thought of that," Bunny admitted. "After wrapping packages all day, any job looks fascinating. You know what I dream of at night?"

"Dan Harding?" Kay suggested impishly.

"Honestly, Kay!" Bunny protested, her cheeks turning pink. "I dream of brown paper—acres of it."

"Cheer up, you won't be wrapping packages all your life," Kay consoled. "At least, they've practically promised it'll be steady work."

Kay was right. That Saturday, Bunny was spared the nervous trip to Miss Callendar's desk. Miss Holly informed her that they expected enough work to keep her busy for the remainder of vacation.

That week end Bunny had another date with Dan, this time to go dancing. So far she hadn't been able to save anything from her paychecks. Last week it had been clothes to wear to work. This week she bought a new dance dress with matching shoes and purse.

The dance was at the civic auditorium, downtown. The night was warm and couples jostled elbow to elbow.

"What do you mean by pulling a disappearing act?" Dan accused her as they circled the floor. "I was in Paradine's today. I went down to that cave with all the plastic dishpans and sink pumps, but you had vanished."

Bunny's eyes twinkled at his description of housewares. "Oh, I got swept out by one of the brooms. I haven't been in housewares for two weeks."

Dan's smile faded. "Don't tell me I got you fired?"

Bunny shook her head. "No, they moved me to another department."

"Which one, so I'll know where to find you?"

Bunny hated to admit that she had been demoted. "I'm still in the basement, but I'm a slave in brown paper now," she said glumly.

"You make it sound like the end of the world," Dan chided. "What do you do?"

Bunny hesitated. To tell him she spent most of her time wrapping packages sounded rather dreary. Dan wasn't the kind of person who liked dreary conversations. "Oh, I tie ribbons and bows and sometimes I help Inez DeWitt."

"Not Miss DeWitt of the sugary television voice?" Dan asked admiringly. "Sounds like you're pretty important."

"So important they move me to a new department every two weeks?" Bunny asked with a wry smile.

He chuckled. "Maybe they're grooming you for something big. My uncle owns a factory in Los Angeles. Instead of giving my cousin a fancy office job when he got out of school, he made him an errand boy. That way he gets to know all the departments. They say that's the trend nowadays for training top personnel."

Bunny smiled gratefully. He had a knack for making one feel ten feet tall.

Later, he spotted a couple he knew at college. "Do you go to JC, too?" the girl asked Bunny.

"Bunny works at Paradine's. She's an assistant to Inez DeWitt," Dan explained grandly.

"Dan, really!" Bunny tried to protest, but no one paid any attention. The other couple looked impressed, especially the girl. Bunny recognized the dress she was wearing. It came from Paradine's—a green imitation-linen sheath that cost fifteen dollars in misses' ready-to-wear. Bunny's tangerine sundress with the spaghetti straps and embroidered jacket came from the Campus Shop and cost twenty-five dollars. For some strange reason this secret knowledge helped her self-confidence.

The following week, Kay's lunch hours were changed, and they no longer were able to eat together except on Saturdays. Bunny couldn't afford to eat at Suffolk's Drugstore with some of the younger girls. This last week she had bought some slacks for a bowling date with Dan, and there had been that simply fabulous sale on imported mohair sweaters. For the first time, she was rather lonely.

Then, the second week in August, Miss Holly was talking with a strange girl when Bunny came to work. "Taylor, this is Anna Finch. I guess you know the routine well enough to help her get started."

Bunny looked at the girl, who was nervously unfolding her blue smock. She was a little shorter than herself, with a stocky build and short brown hair worn in a casual flip style. She was not particularly pretty, but she had a fresh, scrubbed look. Most important, she was about Bunny's age.

"Hello, Anna," Bunny said, feeling very important. Of course, Cheri was on vacation this week, but Miss Holly must have thought she had done pretty well to give her the responsibility of breaking in a new girl.

"I hope I don't make some horrible mistake," Anna confided once they were alone.

"You won't," Bunny assured her. "The work is easy. You don't use a cash register, make out sales slips or do any of the things you learned in the training class."

"What training class? I learned how to use a cash register along with typing and shorthand in my business course in high school," Anna said.

Bunny looked surprised. "I thought all relief workers had to take the training class."

"I'm not a relief worker. I'm a permanent employee. At least, I hope I am." Anna held up crossed fingers. Bunny learned that she had graduated from Northside High School that June. Afterward her family had gone on a six-week vacation. As a result, by the time Anna returned to Bolton, other June graduates had claimed the better jobs. She wasn't interested in sales work. Someday she hoped to work in the office at Paradine's, but for now the job in the wrapping department was all that was available.

Like Bunny on her first day, Anna had planned

to eat in restaurants. Bunny explained how this gobbled up one's paycheck and took her to the employee's lunchroom. "The 10 per cent employees' discount is the other temptation you have to watch," she warned. She gestured helplessly. "Look at who's talking! I've worked here almost eight weeks and I haven't saved a penny!"

Anna leaned across the table with a conspiratorial laugh. "I know what you mean. I've already spent my first check a dozen ways—a set of artist's oils for my sister, a black slip for Mom, a pipe for Dad and something completely dreamy and wild for me, just to prove I'm on my way in the big world."

Bunny's face glowed. She liked Anna better every minute. "I bought a chemistry set for my brother, a blouse for my mother, and a forty-dollar beach outfit for myself," she confided.

"A forty-dollar beach outfit!" Anna clamped pink hands to her mouth. "That was really wild!"

On Saturday, when she joined them for lunch, Kay seemed to like Anna, too. That first week while she was learning the routine, Anna was rather quiet, but once she began to relax she chattered constantly. She and Bunny found a hundred things in common, from liking the same pop bands to favorite actors and banana nut ice cream. They shopped together and tried to be a good influence on each other. They each managed to save a little out of one paycheck, then blew all of it by staying downtown one evening for dinner and attending a first-run movie. The remaining weeks of summer passed quickly.

"One more week and Bunny and I will be going back to school," Kay observed one Saturday.

"Gosh, I'm going to miss you," Anna said.

"We'll stop in now and then to buy a hankie," Kay promised.

"In the wrapping department?" Anna hooted. "You'll have to order it by mail, and I'll seal it with a kiss."

For once Bunny did not join in their laughter. Where had the months gone? She had learned more this summer than she had in all of her years in high school.

"You're wanted upstairs in Personnel," Miss Holly told Bunny on Monday morning.

Bunny glanced at Anna with puzzled eyes. There was no reason she should be called to the office until Saturday, when she picked up her final check. On the fourth floor, nods from Miss Callendar and Mrs. Kearns's secretary propelled her along to the inner office. Today, Mrs. Kearns wore a lime suit with a touch of black braid and chunky black stone earrings. She looked more unapproachable than ever.

"I hardly know whether to consider you a permanent or a part-time employee, you've worked with us so steadily," she began once Bunny had been seated.

Bunny responded to that magical smile, though by now she had a strong suspicion that Mrs.

Kearns turned it on and off like a light switch. "I wish I was a permanent employee," she confided.

"That is what I wanted to talk to you about," Mrs. Kearns said. "One of your co-workers, Cheri Mays, has just given us notice that she is leaving on the fifteenth. That means we're going to be short in the wrapping department just at the time of year when things are picking up. Miss Holly reports that your work has been satisfactory. If you haven't made other plans, I was wondering if you would care to stay on."

Bunny felt the room spinning around her. They were asking her to stay. This could be her chance to start up the ladder in a big company.

"I can give you a couple of days to think it over," Mrs. Kearns offered.

Bunny thought of her mother. There would be a terrible argument, but she couldn't tell the personnel manager that she had to ask her mother's permission. One didn't need a high school education to know that an employer expected you to make your own decisions. "I don't have to think it over. I'd like the job. Of course, I'd really prefer . . . sales work?" Her voice lifted hopefully.

Mrs. Kearns's smile faded. "I'm afraid we don't have any openings right now in sales work," she said.

"Oh, I'm very happy in the wrapping department. Maybe later I can work up to something else," Bunny hastened to say.

"Yes, I hope you can," Mrs. Kearns replied

automatically. Her eyes already were returning to her work. "Before you leave, my secretary will give you another form to fill out."

Bunny rose. It was plain that she was being dismissed. At the door, Mrs. Kearns's voice stopped her. "Just one minute."

Bunny's heart stuck in her throat. Maybe the personnel director had changed her mind?

Mrs. Kearns turned on the magic smile again. "We are very glad to have you with us, Miss Taylor."

Bunny filled out the form for the secretary and floated blithely down the hall to the elevator. Miss Holly seemed relieved when she learned Bunny would be staying with them. Anna stifled a squeal of delight. "How wonderful! Now we'll be working together." Her face clouded. "What about your mother, though? Isn't she expecting you to go back to school?"

Bunny wished that cold, bleak feeling would stop trying to elbow into her happiness. She remembered that long-ago conversation with Sandy. "You have to go ahead and prove you're right," her chum had advised.

"My mother won't like it, but I'm over sixteen," she told Anna.

Anna's gray eyes were admiring. "You've got nerve. My folks would never have let me quit school." In spite of the brave front, Bunny's hands trembled slightly as she pasted a label on a package. She wished she did not have to face her mother tonight.

That evening she and Anna ran into Kay as they were leaving the store. Kay refused to share her enthusiasm. "I think you're making a terrible mistake," she said bluntly. "I hope you won't make any final decision until you've talked it over with your mother."

"She's just jealous," Anna consoled Bunny when Kay had gone. "While she's fooling around with a lot of useless classes, you'll be getting ahead. Next summer, she'll be a part-time worker again and you'll have had a promotion."

Bunny hoped Anna was right, but as she rode home on the bus she knew that she should never have given Mrs. Kearns an answer without consulting her mother first. This was her big chance, surely her own mother wouldn't stand in the way.

The argument that night was worse than Bunny had feared. It started when Mrs. Taylor came home from work and continued on through dinner and afterwards, when the dishes were done and Doug had fled to his room. To Bunny's despair, her mother wouldn't listen to her arguments.

"I've already told them I'll take the job," she cried.

"You had no right to do that. You'll just have to tell them you changed your mind," Mrs. Taylor replied.

"You can't ask me to do that!" Bunny's voice trembled on the verge of tears. "Can't you see you're asking me to give up my chance of a lifetime?"

"Working as a wrapping clerk—you call that a chance of a lifetime?"

Bunny winced at the sarcasm. Maybe it wasn't the greatest job in the world, but it wasn't playing fair when someone you loved hurt you. Suddenly she had a desire to lash back. "It's better than your first job, pressing pants in a tailor shop!"

"I didn't have any choice," her mother replied. "That's why I intend to keep you in school. I wasn't able to finish high school, but thirty years ago thousands of other young people were in the same fix, and it wasn't so important. Nowadays, there isn't any excuse for a person not finishing her education. Most places require a diploma before they'll even consider giving you a job. I'm actually surprised at Paradine's . . . unless they don't know?"

Bunny drew herself up loftily and played what she hoped was her winning card. "They know, and they don't care. Your ideas are old-fashioned. Paradine's is a big, modern store. They do things the modern way. It doesn't matter to them that I don't have a diploma."

"In that case, I think my ideas are more modern than Paradine's," Mrs. Taylor replied. "Now, I don't want to hear any more. You're returning to school."

Once Bunny had stood a little in awe of her mother, but these last months she had been ex-

posed to more successful career women, like Mrs.
Kearns and Miss DeWitt. She seemed to be seeing
her mother in a new perspective. Her mother no
longer was the chic, poised executive. She was
just a tired-looking, middle-aged woman who dyed
her hair and wore tight girdles to look young and
lived two decades behind the rest of the world in
her thinking. Bunny had a weak, frightened feeling, like she was balanced on a precipice. As much
as she loved her mother, she couldn't let someone
like her ruin her life. "I won't go back to school,"
she said in a stubborn voice. "I'm over sixteen, and
no one can make me."

"You're under twenty-one, I'm your legal
guardian and I can make you," Mrs. Taylor replied
in an equally determined tone.

"I won't stay in school."

"I'll notify the truant officer, in that case."

Bunny drew a deep, painful breath and leaped
from the precipice. "You can force me to sit
through every class, but you can't force me to
study. I'm already getting poor grades. I won't
pass. You can make me waste nine months, but I
still won't graduate. Or you can let me go to work
and do something useful with my time."

Mrs. Taylor's eyes were hard and searching. "In
other words, you're threatening me. Is this a kind
of blackmail?"

Bunny gripped the sink until her knuckles
turned white. "Oh, dear God," she sent up a little
prayer. "Make Mom understand, make her stop

71

looking at me like that!" Something deep inside cried out for her to give in, to do anything to wipe that condemning look off her mother's face. But she kept her eyes steady and held her chin high. "I'm sorry if that's the way it sounds, Mom, but I can't let you ruin my life."

"I'm afraid you don't give me much choice. Either way you seem to be asking that I ruin it," Mrs. Taylor replied. She let out a long sigh. "All right, keep this job. Leave school. You're still very young. Maybe you'll discover your mistake in time." Turning on her heel, she went into the other room, where she clicked on the television and threw herself heavily into a chair.

Bunny's tense fingers relaxed their hold on the sink. It was over. She had won. She ran to their bedroom. The strain of the battle had been too great. She burst into tears and muffled her face in the pillow.

When the sobs had subsided, she felt better. Rolling onto her back, she began to make plans. Her mother would be angry for a few days, but she would get over it. In time she would see how wise the decision had been. Bunny took a bath and manicured her nails. It was ten-thirty when her mother came in and silently started getting undressed.

Bunny propped herself on one elbow in her twin bed. "I'm sorry we had to fight," she apologized. "But you'll see that I'm right. You can't say that I'm being selfish, either. With me working and helping with expenses, things will be a lot easier for you."

"The same way that you have made them easier these last three months?" Mrs. Taylor replied in a cutting voice.

Bunny rolled over. Never before in her life had she felt so frightened and alone. It was as though the last thin line of communication between herself and her mother had been severed forever. But she would show her. She would show everyone!

6

Career Girl

The following morning, Bunny and her mother achieved what appeared to be a truce. They did not mention the quarrel again. Doug, wrapped in his own boyish interests, apparently did not notice any difference, but Bunny knew it was there. It was as though both were afraid to open the subject again for fear things might be said that never could be taken back.

That week end Bunny called her friends. "Bunny, I knew you'd have the gumption." Sandy's voice was elated. "I told you that sometimes you just have to stand up to your parents."

Pam and Eileen were equally surprised. "Golly, Bunny, I don't know what to say." Pam's voice was oddly shocked. "I mean, it's wonderful and all that, but don't you think . . . ? Well, my goodness!" For a girl as smart as Pam, it was a rather unintelligent remark.

But nothing could dampen Bunny's enthusiasm particularly on Monday morning, when the high school students started back to their classes. As she waited for the bus, she was aware of them passing in groups on the sidewalk, carrying their new notebooks. She felt grown-up and superior. Here she was, as young as many of them, and already started on her career.

That first week passed in a happy aura of excitement, except for Dan's telephone call on Wednesday night. He'd had to cancel their last date because of some affair that had come up at the college. Now, his voice was even more apologetic.

"I'm sorry I didn't call sooner, but I've really been swamped this week—with registration and everything," he said.

"Sure, I understand. I've been busy, too," Bunny told him.

"I'd really like to see you," he continued, "but I'm being rushed by this fraternity. Saturday they're giving some big doings. Then Sunday I have to hit the books. After that I have to be thinking about starting basketball practice." He didn't sound like himself; his voice had an odd nervousness.

Small cold fingers seemed to be stealing around Bunny's heart. "Sure, I understand," she repeated in a voice that seemed to be stuck like a phonograph needle.

"Well, that's swell." Dan sounded relieved now. "Well, be seeing you."

Bunny hung up the receiver and that cold, bleak feeling encased her heart completely. She knew she would not be seeing Dan again. Now that he was back in school, he had other interests. It had been fun, but one of those summer friendships that end as quickly as they begin.

September brought the last spell of summer heat. By mid-October the plane trees along the boulevard were shedding their crackling leaves and the night breezes that crept up from the river carried a cold, dripping marsh fog. Bunny had saved forty dollars from her September wages. Instead of opening a savings account as her mother suggested, Bunny splurged and made a down payment on an expensive cashmere coat with a real mink collar.

The honey-colored coat could keep out the chill of the fog, but it was no protection against that new feeling of loneliness. There began to be a dreary sameness about her work. She missed Dan and Kay, too. Anna was nice, but when you were with a person eight hours a day you were bound to run out of conversation. Sandy was wrapped up in her impending motherhood. Pam and Eileen were busy with school.

One Saturday evening when the telephone rang, Bunny leaped to grab it. For some silly reason she had hoped that it might be Dan, but Pam's lively voice was almost as good.

"Are you doing anything tonight?" Pam asked.

"No; any wild suggestions?" Bunny's voice was almost too eager. Across the room, her mother lowered her magazine and watched with troubled eyes.

"Eileen's here. Come over and we'll think of something," Pam invited.

"Be there in five minutes." Bunny banged down the receiver and turned to her mother. "Is it all right if I go over to Pam's?"

Mrs. Taylor nodded and glanced toward the darkened window. "I'll have Doug walk over with you."

Bunny gave her an exasperated look. It was only four blocks to Pam's house. She wondered if her mother would ever start treating her like an adult.

At the last minute, she changed back into the red wool dress that she had worn to work. She touched up her makeup and wiggled her arms into the new cashmere coat.

It was obvious that Doug didn't look forward to the walk any more than she did. Bunny persuaded him to turn back at Pam's corner.

Mrs. Parmenter opened the door. "Bunny, I hardly recognized you. How grown-up you look!" she cried.

Eileen came down the hall in a plaid skirt and sloppy sweater. Pam, even more casually dressed, trailed behind.

"Bunny, you didn't need to get all dressed up," Pam said. "What a gorgeous coat."

"Oh, these are just the clothes I wear to work," Bunny said casually.

"And look at your hair!" Eileen cried when they were in Pam's room. "It looks lighter or more grown-up or something."

Bunny smiled. "I wear it this way at the store to make me look older," she explained.

"Honest, Bunny, I can't get over it," Pam said. "I mean, your dropping out of school and all."

"It looks like it agrees with you," Eileen added.

"It does. I love it," Bunny told them.

There was an awkward silence. "What do you hear from Sandy?" Eileen asked.

"Not much," Bunny admitted. "She's awfully busy with plans for the baby."

"I know. You'd think she invented mother-hood," Pam said with a laugh.

There was another pause. "Well, tell me all the news from school," Bunny invited.

Eileen was dating Grover McQuire now. Pam had a divine English teacher who thought she had real talent for poetry. The skits at the Girls' Hi Jinx were going to be hilarious.

Bunny listened politely. Grover What's-His-Name was new this year, as was the English teacher. And she always had thought the Hi Jinx skits were silly.

Around eight o'clock Pam and Eileen finally ran down. "Now, tell us what you have been doing." Eileen said.

"Well, I got to help Inez DeWitt again this week," Bunny began.

"Inez Who?" Eileen's voice was vague.

"Dummy. She's the lady shopper you see on the Paradine's television show," Pam explained disgustedly. She smiled at Bunny. "Golly, that sounds fabulous. You really must be getting ahead."

Bunny realized abruptly that while Pam was trying to appear interested, neither of them really cared about the recent happenings at Paradine's Department Store.

"Look, we've talked, now let's do something," she suggested. "What about a show? There's a good comedy at the Southside."

Pam and Eileen shook their heads. "Remember, we're on allowances," Pam said mournfully. "I even cut out Cokes this week to save for my Hi Jinx costume."

Eileen nodded. "And I'm saving for a ticket to the Girls' League Dance. I'm inviting Grover."

There was a long silence.

"Why don't we go to the Youth Center?" Pam suggested. "There's always a gang there. We can dance or listen to the records."

Even Bunny nodded eagerly. The Youth Center was fun. Best of all, it was free.

It was only two blocks from Pam's house to the center, which was located across the street from the park in an old-fashioned cement building that had once housed a branch library. As they drew closer, they could hear the sound of music and see the shadows moving against the lighted windows.

They fell in behind a group of boys going up the steps. A tall, dark boy, wearing a Northside sweater, stood in the doorway. Reaching automatically into their purses, Pam and Eileen found their student-body cards. Simultaneously, all of their faces went blank. "Oh, my gosh! We forgot Bunny doesn't have . . ." Pam's voice broke off in confusion.

"Okay, keep moving. Show your cards," the boy directed in an authoritative voice.

"She forgot hers," Pam nodded toward Bunny. "You will let her in, won't you?"

The boy's eyes swept Bunny. Apparently he took his job seriously. "Sorry, but you know the rules. You have to have your card for identification."

The girls withdrew a short distance for consultation. "Bunny, I feel awful," Pam apologized. "I completely forgot those silly rules."

"It's not your fault," Bunny replied. "I should have remembered."

Turning, she went back to the door. "I have last year's card. Won't that do?" Fumbling in her wallet, she found her old student-body card.

The boy hesitated, looking from the card to her. "It doesn't look much like you."

"Silly, that's because she's doing her hair differently," Pam put in.

"Well. . . ." He seemed to be weakening.

"What seems to be the trouble?" One of the chaperones, a thin-faced man of about forty, joined them.

Looking relieved, the boy nodded at Bunny. "She hasn't a current card, but she found last year's."

The man glanced from the card to Bunny. Without a smile, he handed it back. "Sorry, young lady, we made those rules for your own protection. If we make one exception we have to make another. Since you come from the high school right in this district, it shouldn't be far for you to go home and get your card."

Seconds later, a group of young people had elbowed them out of the doorway. "What a bunch of squares," Eileen said with a sniff, but her eyes returned longingly to the doorway. "Grover's here. I could have introduced you."

"We can go back to my house and make some cocoa," Pam suggested rather unenthusiastically as they stopped on the bottom step.

"Look, we had a nice visit. You two go on inside. I'll go home," Bunny said.

"Bunny, we couldn't do that!" Pam and Eileen protested in unison.

Bunny looked up at the doorway again, at a bunch of silly, immature school kids, gangling boys, giggling girls. "Sure you can," she insisted. "I'm tired anyhow."

"It's not fair," Pam continued to protest.

"We can at least walk you home." Eileen was the first to give in.

"I don't need anyone to walk me home." Bunny tried not to sound irritable. Then she smiled and patted both their shoulders. "Honest, I don't mind. Have fun. I'll call you one of these days." Seconds later, she was hurrying away in the fog.

Pam and Eileen didn't follow. She really hadn't expected them to. In the drifting fog, with the street lights reduced to blurry stars, the streets seemed suddenly dark and lonely. Bunny walked very fast.

"You're home early," her mother said when she reached the apartment.

"We talked for awhile, then Pam and Eileen wanted to go to the Youth Center."

Mrs. Taylor frowned. "You should have gone with them."

Bunny shrugged. "Dance with that bunch of infants? No thanks."

"Besides, you don't have a student-body card anymore, so you couldn't have gotten in," Doug spoke up suddenly.

Bunny glared at him furiously, wondering why she had to be burdened with a smart-aleck, thirteen-year-old brother. As she started down the hall, she noticed that troubled look in her mother's eyes again.

After that there didn't seem to be much point in trying to get together with Pam and Eileen. Anna didn't have a steady boyfriend. The following week, she and Bunny stayed downtown after work and had dinner at Charmaine's and went to a show. It was the first of many similar evenings. One time they ate at a seafood place, another time they tried a French restaurant.

At Christmas, things picked up. Like most of the downtown stores, Paradine's remained open evenings during most of December. To handle the increase in business all the regular relief workers were called in along with dozens of extra holiday employees. Anna was put in charge of the evening shift in the wrapping department with four other girls working under her, but Bunny was not jealous. Because of her previous experience, she was sent upstairs to hosiery again.

Mary Benson was among those called back for the holidays. She hadn't changed except for the new diamond solitaire on her left hand. Her fiancé was ten years her senior. "But he's got a steady job, and a girl can't sit around home forever," she said.

Bunny frowned and tried to imagine someone marrying because of boredom.

"You ought to try the skating rink, too. You might meet someone," Mary advised.

Bunny hid her irritation. Maybe these last months had been a bit lonely, but she wasn't that desperate.

On Christmas Eve the store closed early for the annual employee's Christmas party. Anna and Bunny took the elevator to the fourth floor, where they found a cold buffet attractively arranged on a long table. Through the doorway to the lunchroom, Bunny could see a few couples dancing. When they had finished eating, Anna got into a conversation with a girl from the business office, while Bunny fidgeted restlessly, her eyes straying toward the dancers. Unfortunately, female employees outnumbered males nearly eight to one.

"You look like a girl who is waiting for someone to ask her to dance," a masculine voice teased at her elbow.

Startled, Bunny looked up at a tall young man in a charcoal gray suit. He had dark hair, a thin, rather aristocratic nose and hazel eyes that seemed to be regarding her with secret amusement.

She blushed. She had not known that her eagerness was so apparent. "Thank you, I'd like to," she replied stiffly.

He didn't say any more, just slid his arm around her waist and led her into the lunchroom. He was a marvelous dancer. At first, Bunny had trouble following his intricate steps; then as her nervousness vanished she found herself enjoying it. Her partner grinned. "I knew it. I told myself you were the only girl in this room that could dance. It's a gift, you know, spotting a blond who has feathers in her feet instead of her head."

Bunny studied him for a minute, not sure whether this was a compliment or not. He seemed very sure of himself. "In that case, I suppose I should be flattered," she said a bit tartly.

He chuckled and introduced himself. "I'm George Presser from men's shoes. I've been watching you since you came in. In this roomful of female antiques you stand out like Snow White among seventy-seven dwarfs."

Bunny laughed in spite of herself. She learned that George had been working at Paradine's over a year. He was twenty-two and unmarried. "I'm looking, though." His eyes warmed noticeably. "Where has old Matthew Paradine been keeping you tucked away that we haven't run into each other before?"

Bunny explained that she usually worked in the wrapping department.

"You mean they hide you down in the basement tying ribbons all day?" he protested.

"Oh, we do other things beside gift wrapping," Bunny said. "We handle all the packages that go through the mail."

His eyes twinkled. "I get it. That's where you play games of interoffice post office. Say, how do I get transferred to that department?"

Bunny found herself blushing again.

George stopped dancing. Arm around her waist, he steered her off the floor. "C'mon, you can stand one more cup of punch. Let's find someplace to talk."

The best spot they could find was the bench outside the personnel office, but it was better than nothing. Suddenly George's face was earnest. "I'm sorry if I seem to be rushing things. Really, I'm not that kind of a guy. It's just that waiting on a bunch of big-footed oafs eight hours a day, forty hours a week, can be a lonesome business. You don't have a chance to meet any girls. Then I look across the room tonight, and there you are. You've been working right here in the same store all these months. . . ."

Bunny warned herself that he could be handing her an awfully smooth line, yet his feelings were so exactly like her own that she felt herself responding. They talked a while longer, then danced again. George had ambitions. He expected to be promoted to assistant manager of men's shoes before long. Someday, he hoped to be manager-buyer of all men's wear.

Mr. Paradine did not believe in office parties that lasted all evening and kept working people from their families. Shortly before eight, people started drifting home. Bunny found it hard to believe that two hours had gone so quickly. "Of course you're going to let me take you home," George said.

Until then, Bunny had almost forgotten Anna, who had so carefully arranged for their family car for that evening. "I'm sorry, but I've already made arrangements." For a dismal moment, she saw the episode of Dan repeating itself.

But George did not have Dan's schoolboy improvidence. "You don't expect me to lose you again when I've just found you," he said, taking out an address book. "Give me your telephone number, and I'll call you tomorrow."

Bunny's heart turned cartwheels as she watched him write it down.

"It was a pretty good party. At least they had plenty of food," Anna observed as she drove Bunny home.

Bunny gazed out of the window at a sky so clear she could almost touch the stars. Tonight, instead of being accompanied by its usual cold gray fog, the breeze from the river was dry and crisp with excitement. "It was a wonderful party!" she corrected.

"So I noticed," Anna teased. "He was good-looking, too."

The following day was Christmas. For Doug, Bunny had purchased an aquarium complete with tropical fish; for her mother, a velveteen lounging robe with pearl trim. Both were expensive gifts, and she was glad when her mother thanked her graciously and made no comment about the price. During the afternoon, George called as he had promised. The following night he attended night school, but on Friday he invited her to stay downtown for dinner and a show.

The next day, Bunny was lucky enough to get an afterwork appointment at the beauty shop. It was after eight before the bus let her off at the corner. A scarf protecting her new set, she bounded up the steps to the apartment.

Her mother was not alone. A youthful, energetic-looking woman in a gray squirrel coat was seated on the sofa. There was something vaguely familiar about her face. "Hello, Bunny, I'm Miss Carmichael, one of your student counselors from South Bolton High," she introduced herself.

Puzzled, Bunny took off her scarf and coat. Just the mention of school had caused a cramped feeling in her throat. "Didn't Mom tell you? I don't go to high school anymore," she said.

Miss Carmichael's voice was unruffled. "Yes, I know. That's really the reason why I am here. I'm making a survey of high school dropouts." She explained that the local school authorities were becoming disturbed by the number of young people leaving high school. During Christmas vacation, counselors from the various high schools had volunteered to contact every young person who had dropped out of the local schools in the last three years. The object was to try to discover their reasons for leaving school as well as offer assistance to those who might want to resume their education.

Miss Carmichael smiled. "You'd be surprised at some of the reasons we find for dropouts. Where it's financial, and the young person's wages are needed at home, the best we can suggest is night school. Sometimes, it's just a small thing like a pair of shoes or a decent outfit of clothes. We have service clubs that can supply these. Lack of incentive, poor grades, discipline problems—there are almost as many different reasons as there are different young people."

Her eyes went to Bunny. "It doesn't look like your problem was financial. According to the records, your grades were about average, and you certainly were not a discipline problem."

"I dropped out of school because I felt it was wasting my time," Bunny explained. "It's very nice of you to be interested, but I don't need any help. I have a good job. I've never been happier in my life."

Miss Carmichael did not look angry. She smiled as she drew on her gloves. "You're one of the lucky ones then, Bunny. But they say it takes the exceptions to prove the rule."

At the doorway, she paused. "I hope you'll promise me one thing. If you ever change your mind, remember, I can always be reached through my office at the high school." Bunny watched her go down the steps, a slim gray figure that melted into the fog.

"At least, you could have listened to her," Mrs. Taylor complained.

"I did listen," Bunny protested. "But why waste her time when I don't have any problems?"

7

Don't Call Us . . .

The date with George was everything Bunny had expected. He was good company, and the show was entertaining. Monday, he took her to lunch at Suffolk's Drugstore. The next week end they had another date. They went to a place called The Catamaran, where there were hurricane lamps on the tables, fishnet-draped walls and shifting colored lights that played over the small dance floor. Bunny sipped her soft drink and felt the bubbles travel along the straw and out to her fingertips. It was the first time that she had ever been in a real nightclub. Wait until she told Anna!

"Hold it," George ordered, leaning forward. "I wish I had a picture of you smiling like that. They ought to nominate you Miss Paradine of the year."

It was an outrageous compliment, but she felt a little giddy.

After Christmas, the work in the wrapping department had fallen off to almost nothing. Bunny and Anna had to struggle to look busy. Two days, Bunny was sent upstairs to notions to help while the regular girl was ill. Later, things picked up a little with the January white sale and start of inventory. Bunny spent one morning unpacking sheets, another checking stock for housewares.

Wednesday, she was five minutes late getting away for lunch. George had already gone on to Suffolk's without her. "What kept you so long?" he complained as she slid into the booth.

"I've been all over the store this morning," Bunny explained. "I'm beginning to feel like everyone's Girl Friday."

"Girl Tuesday, you mean. You aren't old enough to be a Girl Friday," he teased.

Bunny scowled at him across the rim of her glass. "I'm not that young!" she protested.

"C'mon," he chuckled, "you aren't a day over nineteen."

With painful effort, Bunny swallowed a mouthful of water. If he thought nineteen was young, what would he think if he knew her real age?

"What does your mother think of George?" Anna asked later.

"At first, she thought he was a little old, but now that she's found out that he goes to night school, she likes him." Bunny made a face. "I think it's an obsession with her. I could bring home a boy with green hair and two heads and she would like him if he were going to school."

Anna laughed. "That's probably because she still hopes you'll go back. Once you get a promotion, it'll be different. I suppose you've heard the rumor. Once inventory's over there's supposed to be some kind of reorganization. I'm hoping it will be my chance for an office job."

"Maybe I'll be transferred to sales work," Bunny agreed eagerly.

With everyone busy with inventory, Bunny did not see much of George the next few days. She was glad when Friday came to a close. All day, there had been a horrid, sticky feeling in her throat, as though she were coming down with a cold.

The next morning, she awoke with a head that seemed to be stuffed with hot cotton. Her mother was sympathetic but firm. "You're lucky that it's Saturday. If you take some aspirin and gargle you should be able to make it through one more day. Then Sunday you can rest."

As Bunny rode downtown in the chill, gray morning, she didn't feel lucky. She couldn't help thinking that if she had been in school she probably would have been allowed to stay home.

As the day progressed, she felt worse. Wrapping a simple shower gift became a monumental task. Ribbons twisted, tape refused to stick. By closing time, she was so miserable she was ready to cry.

"You look awful. You better rush right home and crawl into bed," Anna advised.

"Thab's just whab I'm gudda do," Bunny mumbled thickly and blew her nose. But there was something that she had to do first. She hadn't seen George for three days, but when they'd had lunch Wednesday he'd hinted at a date this week end.

When she had squirmed into her coat, she hurried to the Elm Street entrance. Outside it had begun to rain. Clerks and salesgirls swept past her, letting in gusts of chill air as they pushed through the swinging doors. Bunny leaned against the wall and tried to keep her teeth from chattering.

At last she saw him. He was with two other men and so busy talking that he might have passed without seeing her if she hadn't called his name. "Bunny, what are you doing here?" he asked.

"I've got a terrible cold. I thought I'd bedder led you know . . . I mean, if you were pladdig on coming by . . . ?" Suddenly, she felt embarrassed. She shouldn't have waited for him here. She should have gone home and let him phone her if he really wanted that date. She had wanted so desperately to do the right thing.

To her relief, his eyes were concerned. "Poor kid, you do look sick," he sympathized. "Forget this week end. I have something I ought to do anyhow. You go on home and get some rest." Joining his friends, he waved from the door.

Bunny did not know why there should be that sinking feeling in her chest. She guessed for a moment she had hoped that he might offer to drive her home. Outside, the rain cooled her face. She waited fifteen minutes for the bus, then had to stand half the way home. By the time she stumbled up the apartment steps, she had a temperature of 102°.

The next day, Bunny felt no better, and her mother had to get the doctor. Monday, Mrs. Taylor telephoned Paradine's and did not go to work herself until after eleven, when she was certain that Bunny would be all right. It was not until Friday that Bunny returned to work, with her hair badly in need of a set and her nose pink and swollen.

"Did you manage to survive without me?" She tried to make a joke of it as she greeted Anna.

"We survived," Anna agreed. "In fact, things were so slow I was tempted to wrap every package twice just to look busy."

Anna had telephoned twice while Bunny was ill, but there had not been a single call from George. Bunny tried to ignore that nagging, worried feeling. Work was so slow that she and Anna were able to take their lunch break together.

Bunny saw George the moment she came through the lunchroom door. He was not alone. Bunny could not see his companion's face, only that she had honey-blond hair and was wearing an electric-blue knit dress with a lot of crystal beads at her throat. Their heads were almost touching.

Glancing up, he saw Bunny in the doorway. He

grinned and lifted his hand casually before he turned back to his companion.

Bunny seemed to be turning hollow inside. She told herself that George could eat with whomever he pleased. He had made no promises. Her face fixed in a bright, false smile, she made her way to a table.

Anna brought hot chocolate for both of them. She seemed to read Bunny's thoughts. "He's been with her every day this week. She's from cosmetics. I heard he took her to Suffolk's on Wednesday. Golly, Bunny, I hope you're not going to mind."

Bunny took a swallow of cocoa so hot that she almost choked. "Why should I mind?" she inquired lightly. It was a lie. She did mind. Her pride felt like it had been hit with a sledgehammer. She thought of all those compliments. He'd made her believe she was something very special.

Anna's eyes returned to the couple across the room. Their heads were even closer now and George was smiling. "He's probably telling her she should be Miss Paradine of the year," she observed scathingly.

Bunny lowered her cup with a hand that shook. "Where did you get that idea?" she sputtered.

Anna shrugged. "From Zelda Frees. I ate with her one day while you were sick. He tried to give Zelda the rush about six months ago. She says he tries that line on every girl in the store."

Bunny thought of how she had waited for him last Saturday. As though she were chasing after him

96

like some silly, lovesick schoolgirl. She wanted to die from shame. It was an effort to maneuver her face back into a sunny, uncaring smile. Those next days she kept busy, and she pretended not to notice the silly way George Presser was running after the blond from cosmetics.

The last Friday in January, Anna was summoned to the office. When she returned, Bunny could tell by her shining eyes that something tremendous had happened. "Those rumors were true. They are reorganizing the department and you'll never guess what. . . ." Her voice trailed away. Mrs. Ashford was ringing for help at the counter. "Tell you at lunch." Anna ducked through the door.

Bunny could hardly wait until noon. If George was seated somewhere in the lunchroom with his new interest, she couldn't have cared less. According to Anna, the mailing and wrapping department was being combined with the shipping department into a single unit. "Miss Holly is being made assistant to the man who is the head of shipping now. Mrs. Ashford will still be in charge of the gift-wrapping counter, but it's being moved upstairs next to the service desk. She and Inez DeWitt are going to share a secretary-assistant, and guess who it's going to be?" Anna didn't wait for Bunny to guess. "Me! I'll type Miss DeWitt's correspondence and help Mrs. Ashford the rest of the time."

Bunny stared at her, open-mouthed. Secretary to

Inez DeWitt, even if it only was part-time, sounded beyond belief. "That's wonderful, Anna, simply wonderful!" The words managed to come out, but deep inside it was impossible not to feel that sickening stab of jealousy. She had been at Paradine's longer than Anna. She should have had that promotion!

Bunny wondered if her face always gave her away. "It's probably because I've had typing and shorthand," Anna explained. "But you wait. They're calling everyone up to the office. You'll do all right."

Bunny's spirits lifted. That had to be it. They must be transferring her to sales work.

She was not called to the office until Saturday, an hour before closing time. With trembling fingers, Bunny hung the blue apron on a hook, patted her hair and headed for the elevator. As she was carried upward, her hands were like ice.

Mrs. Kearns was talking on the telephone, but she nodded toward a chair. Then, as she laid down the receiver, her smile faded.

"I imagine you have already heard that in the interests of economy, we are making the wrapping and mailing department a part of shipping. It's a change that should have been made long ago. Unfortunately, as in all economy moves, it means some of our employees are going to have to be let go."

She leaned forward and regarded Bunny sympathetically. "It is always difficult to tell an employee whose work has been satisfactory that she is no longer needed. I'm very sorry, Miss Taylor, but you are one of the employees whom we are going to have to release."

Stunned, Bunny stared at her. "I don't understand."

Mrs. Kearns's voice was patient as she explained that, between the reorganization and the seasonal dropoff that always followed Christmas and inventory, there simply was no longer enough work to keep Bunny busy.

Somehow, Bunny dragged herself out of benumbed shock. "But I've been here six months. One of the girls who has only been here three got a promotion!"

Mrs. Kearns frowned. "You mean Miss Finch? My dear, I'm afraid there really is no similarity between you. Miss Finch joined us in August as a permanent employee. She's had business training and is a high school graduate. On the other hand, you applied as summer relief worker. Our policy is to employ only high school graduates for our regular staff, though we make exceptions for part-time workers."

Her smile returned. "Speaking of part-time work, I would be very happy to return you to our list of relief workers. I can almost promise that we will be able to call you back for our next sale."

Bunny wanted to scream that they need not bother, that she never wanted to see Paradine's again; but somehow she managed to control the childish surge of rage.

It wasn't until she was out of the office and on her way down the hall to pick up her check and the week's severance pay that they had promised that the horrible truth finally hit her. She hadn't gotten any promotion like Anna. She didn't even have a job any longer. She had been fired!

8

Sorry, Not Hiring

Bunny awoke to rain beating against the window in small gray pellets that melted into rivers of gray tears on the glass. It was Monday morning, but there was no reason to get up. Somewhere behind her, she heard faint rustling sounds as her mother dressed for work.

She had to admit that her mother had been considerate. Not once had she said "I told you so." Sunday she had taken Bunny and Doug out to dinner and a matinee, and no mention had been made of the lost job. But Bunny knew that it must come up sooner or later. When she heard her mother tiptoe back into the room, she closed her eyes and pretended to be asleep.

She waited until the apartment was still and she

thought that both her mother and brother had gone. She slipped into her slippers and robe. The door to Doug's room was ajar, his bed bumpily yanked together with thirteen-year-old abandon. Bunny padded down the hall and stopped in the kitchen doorway in surprise.

Her mother, dressed in her dark suit, still sat at the table. "Good morning, dear," she said brightly, setting down her coffee cup.

"What happened?" Bunny asked. "You always catch the eight forty-five bus."

Mrs. Taylor shrugged. "It's the rain. There won't be many customers today, and Midge has a key to open up. I thought I'd take my time." Her blue eyes met Bunny's in sudden honesty. "Besides, I wanted to know what you were going to do."

Bunny poured a glass of milk and started peeling a banana. "I don't know," she replied uneasily. "I guess I'll just hang around home. It'll be nice getting a little rest."

"You haven't forgotten that Miss Carmichael who came by in December, have you? If the rain lets up a little, you might walk over to the school and talk to her." Mrs. Taylor's voice was hopeful.

Bunny felt the anger start, a hard burning knot in her stomach that spread up her back, stiffening her spine as it progressed. So this was the reason for that sympathy! It had been a ruse to soften her up so that she would return to school. "I don't need to see Miss Carmichael," she said coldly.

"She can't find me a job. All she can do is try to talk me into going back to school."

"It's not such a bad idea," her mother said. "The new semester starts next week."

"South Bolton High doesn't have any February graduating class. What reason would there be to go back now when I couldn't possibly graduate until a year from June?" Bunny asked.

"You could always repeat junior English and bring up your grade or take a couple of special courses like typing or sewing," Mrs. Taylor suggested.

"I already know what I want, and it's not school!" Bunny's voice had a ragged edge of anger. "It's too bad Paradine's let me go, but they said they'd call me back. Meanwhile, I'll look for a better job."

"You may not find one," her mother warned.

"I'll find something!" Bunny cried. "I'm not a baby anymore. Can't everyone realize that and let me alone?"

The anger had spread to her mother's face now. Her lips compressed in a thin line, and she started putting on her raincoat. "In that case, since you seem determined to keep on working, I suggest that you go to the State Department of Employment office this morning. They're at Fourth and Ash. You haven't worked long enough to build up much in unemployment benefits, but you should be eligible for a small check."

"What do I want to see them for?" Bunny

snapped, annoyed because her mother still was insisting on telling her what to do. "I want a job, not relief!"

"The purpose of the Department of Employment is not to hand out relief," Mrs. Taylor explained in the patient voice one might use with a backward child. "They try to bring workers and jobs together. They have listings of openings, and they may be able to help you. If they can't, they'll arrange for your unemployment compensation."

"I found the job with Paradine's without any help; I'll find the next one, too," Bunny replied stubbornly. "Remember? You were the one who said I should do it alone."

For a moment, her mother looked as though she was going to lose her temper. Then abruptly her expression changed. Stepping closer, she kissed Bunny on the cheek. "I hope you're successful, dear," she whispered in a voice that sounded very tired. Then the front door closed behind her.

Bunny rushed to the window in time to see her mother turn up the street, a youthful yet lonely figure in her bright crimson raincoat with her shoulders bent against the storm. She tasted a salty lump in her throat. Already she was ashamed of the spiteful way she had acted. She had an impulse to run after her mother and throw herself sobbing into her arms. Then, returning anger at her own childishness tore her from the window. She wasn't a child any longer. She and her mother had crossed over into a world where they met as grown women now.

Bunny took her breakfast into the living room, where she sprawled on the couch watching television. Gradually, her anger faded. She told herself that she felt a little sorry for Anna and the others at Paradine's. What they wouldn't give to spend a morning dawdling like this! Things really weren't so bad. The job in the wrapping department hadn't been much anyhow. She would take a vacation, then find something better.

The new, comfortable mood was of short duration. By noon, Bunny had grown tired of watching old movies on television. She showered, changed into a sweater and skirt and decided to go downtown. Part of her last paycheck she would keep for spending money; the rest, along with her severance pay, she would put in the bank. That should please her mother.

By now, the rain had stopped; but the sky overhead remained sullen, and there were few people on the bus. Bunny carefully kept to the opposite side of the street from Paradine's as she walked up Eighth Avenue to the bank. It did not take long to complete her business. Afterward, she stopped in front of a dress shop with a display of pastel sweaters in the window. She supposed it was the contrast of the dark day, but their gay, Easter egg colors were like a forecast of spring. The yellow one in particular looked like it was spun out of sunbeams.

Bunny succumbed to temptation and stepped inside. Even the saleswoman agreed the yellow sweater was made for her. "Blonds have to be so careful choosing yellow. The wrong shade can be disaster," she said.

As Bunny waited for her old sweater to be packaged, she was seized with sudden inspiration. "Are you the manager?" she asked.

"Oh, no, that's Mrs. Hudson." The saleswoman nodded toward a stout, dark-haired woman at the rear of the store.

"May I speak to the manager, then?" Bunny asked politely.

The saleswoman's forehead puckered worriedly, but she hurried away.

"Yes, my dear, what can I do for you?" the dark-haired woman beamed at Bunny.

"I noticed that there are only two of you. I was wondering if you might need help. I've had experience—" Bunny began hopefully.

The woman's smile vanished. Small downward lines jerked at her mouth. "No, we don't need anyone. One of my girls is home ill today, the other doesn't come in on Mondays. We're over-staffed now." She turned rudely away.

As Bunny left the store, she told herself that there was no reason for that rejected feeling, she hadn't cared much for Mrs. Hudson either!

On the next corner was Cordel's, one of Bolton's most exclusive shops. Impulsively, Bunny ducked into its luxurious atmosphere of thick rugs, graceful wrought-iron chairs and gilt-edged mirrors.

The girl at the jewelry counter raised stenciled eyebrows. "Mr. Cordel? He never helps on the floor. His office is through that archway at the rear."

Before Bunny reached the archway, a second saleswoman intercepted her. "Mr. Cordel? I'll inquire for you."

She returned, followed by a striking brunette with jeweled glasses who was Mr. Cordel's secretary. "Did you have an appointment?" the secretary drawled.

"No, but I just wanted to inquire about a job," Bunny said.

"Mr. Cordel only interviews applicants who have made appointments," the secretary explained haughtily.

"May I make an appointment then?" Bunny asked.

The secretary's eyes brushed Bunny from head to toe. "I can tell you now you would be wasting your time. Mr. Cordel is not interested in hiring anyone." Those frosty eyes classified Bunny again; this time they seemed amused.

Bunny realized that she never should have come here without an appointment. She should have worn something more fitting than a sweater and skirt. As she left the store, she heard a murmur of voices and subdued tinkle of laughter behind her. Her cheeks flamed.

Outside, it had started to rain again. Bunny did not do anymore job hunting that day but caught the bus home. As she bounded up the apartment stairs, holding the box from the dress shop over her head to ward off the rain, a new worry hit her. What if Paradine's had called while she had been out?

For the next few days, Bunny stayed close to the apartment, hoping there would be a call from Paradine's. Every night she bought a copy of the evening paper and read the want ads. The jobs offered either did not sound very appealing or required experience that she did not have.

Thursday evening Pam called to chat and share the exciting news that she had been elected vice-president of the senior class for the spring semester. "Guess who was my campaign manager?" she said when Bunny offered her congratulations.

"Who?" Bunny inquired.

"Eileen!" Pam shrieked into the telephone. "Can you imagine that? Going with Grover has done it. You know how lazy Eileen used to be? Now she's into everything. She's even lost eight pounds."

Bunny tried to visualize plump, placid Eileen changed into a skinny dynamo. It didn't seem possible that it had been several months since she had seen either of them.

"Listen to me carry on about myself," Pam said suddenly. "How are you getting along with that dreamy job of yours?"

There was a sudden tightness in Bunny's throat.

"I'm not working at Paradine's anymore." She tried to sound casual.

"You're not?" Pam was incredulous.

After the news of Pam's triumph at school, Bunny could not bear to tell her she had been fired. "The job in the wrapping department didn't have much future. Right now I'm taking a little vacation. Then I'm going to look for something better," she explained.

That week end Bunny went to see Sandy. She seemed changed, too, in her maternity smock with her dark hair skinned back in a limp pony tail. She showed Bunny all the things she had bought for the baby. She was learning to knit. As she sank heavily onto the couch, she picked up a prickly bundle of yarn and needles.

With Sandy, who had been her closest chum, Bunny could be honest. She told her about losing her job. "Bunny, that's terrible," Sandy wailed consolingly. Her voice died away, and Bunny saw her lips moving as she counted stitches. Satisfied, she glanced up again. "But honest, Bunny, maybe it's for the best."

Bunny felt herself bristling. "Look, don't give me any lecture about going back to school. I get enough of that at home."

"School—school—who said anything about school?" Sandy replied. Once again there was that maddening interval while she counted stitches. "You ought to get married, Bunny. That's what you ought to do."

"But I don't want to get married yet," Bunny protested.

"Don't be silly. Every girl wants to get married," Sandy insisted complacently. Forehead knotted, she studied her knitting. Then she smiled fondly at Bunny. "Give me your opinion. Do you think Michael Steven or Marshall Stuart would be a prettier name for the baby?"

"Maybe you'll have twins, then you can use both," Bunny said in a tired voice. It was difficult to believe that just a little over a year ago she and Sandy had been chums. Now they had to struggle to find anything in common.

Later, as Bunny waited for the bus, she caught a glimpse of her reflection in a store window: a tall, rather pretty blond girl in a yellow sweater, a girl who didn't look any different from any other seventeen-year-old. But she *was* different. She didn't belong with the school kids like Pam and Eileen. She didn't belong with the settled teen-agers like Sandy. What had happened to her? She didn't belong anywhere.

The following Monday morning, Bunny followed her mother's advice and reported to the office of the Department of Employment, housed in a salmon-colored stucco building at the corner of Ash and Fourth streets. She was surprised at the number of other people who were there. Some were in shabby clothes, others in neat business suits. There were old people, young people, men with sunburned faces who looked like workmen or agricultural workers. There were even a few teen-agers. A stocky boy with dark, brooding eyes seemed indifferent to everything but his own thoughts. A paprika-haired girl, dressed in skin-tight black capris, was talking to a blond boy in a black leather jacket. The girl had a peculiar, pene-trating laugh. Every time the boy said something funny, she would laugh shrilly, and some of the older people would turn to glower with disapprov-al.

The woman who interviewed Bunny was named Mrs. Pierce. She had gray hair, warm brown eyes and a smile that looked as though it would easily ignite into laughter. She asked a lot of questions. By the time Bunny finished answering them, her smile seemed pretty well extinguished. "I'll be quite frank with you, Benecia," she said, using Bunny's given name. "We don't have many calls for teen-agers. The fact that you don't have a high school diploma makes it even more difficult. Most employers require a minimum of a high school education."

"I can't see why a diploma should make any difference," Bunny said. "I have experience."

"A few months of sales work and wrapping packages—I'm afraid the great majority of unem-ployed have that much experience," Mrs. Pierce replied. Her expression brightened. "With jobs so scarce, have you considered going back to school or taking some special training?"

"Never!" Bunny's vehement reply closed that subject.

They talked a few minutes longer, but Mrs. Pierce was not very optimistic. She took Bunny's number and promised to call if something came up. In the meantime, she encouraged Bunny to continue looking on her own. At the end of a week, if she had found nothing, she would be eligible for a small weekly unemployment check.

Bunny left the office feeling disappointed and depressed. A lot of good her mother's advice had been. She might as well not have come at all.

9

Third Time's the Charm

The buds on the plane trees were a hint of yellow-green against the mottled white bark, while in a few gardens paper-white narcissi struggled into premature bloom. Even the bright morning sunlight beating on Bunny's shoulders had a promise of spring. In another week, it would be the first of March. Paradine's had not called. She had not found a job, and the visits to the state employment office were becoming a weekly ritual. By now the faces of some of the others who reported on Monday were becoming familiar: the girl with the paprika-colored hair and her good-looking companion; the middle-aged woman who always wore a purple sweater; the stocky, dark-haired boy.

Today, the stocky boy was ahead of Bunny. He

usually seemed preoccupied with his own thoughts, but this morning when it was his turn to step to the window he gave her a quick smile. "Keep your fingers crossed," he said.

She responded by holding up two fingers. She did not think it brought him luck. If one of the interviewers wanted to see you about a job opening, a marker was attached to your check. The boy had barely stepped to the window before he was turning away again, and it was Bunny's turn.

"Did you look for work this week?" The clerk asked the routine question. Without waiting for Bunny's reply, he already was locating her check. She saw that it had no marker. "It's been three weeks since I had my interview," she said.

"Sorry, we don't have many calls for young people under twenty." He smiled encouragingly. "But keep on trying."

The dark-haired boy had not left. Standing near a bulletin board, he was going through an elaborate routine of folding his check and putting it in his wallet. He fell in beside Bunny as she approached the door.

"No luck for you either?" he asked.

Bunny shook her head. "They said they don't have much call for anyone under twenty."

"But you're to keep on trying," he quoted.

Bunny looked at him in surprise. Then she laughed. "You must know the routine."

"I should," he agreed. "This is my sixth week." He was only a few inches taller than she was, with a square face and determined-looking jaw, but there was something appealing about his lively, dark eyes and thick lashes. Seconds later they were outside, blinking in the bright morning sunlight.

"My name is Tom Costa. I've noticed you here the last couple of weeks. I haven't enough money to keep my car running, so I can't offer you a ride home; but I've enough for a couple of Cokes at the drugstore across the street if you'd care to join me," he invited.

It was more than the February sunlight that brought that warm feeling. Bunny hadn't realized how lonely she had been these last weeks. "I'd love it," she agreed, "but on one condition—I'll buy my own. When you get a job, you can treat me to a banana split."

Tom laughed. "The day I get a job, I'll take you to dinner."

The drugstore on the corner was shabby, the leather tops of the tall stools cracked in places, but somehow that seemed unimportant. It was nice to be talking to someone young again. Bunny learned that Tom was nineteen, going on twenty. He had dropped out of high school three years ago. Since then he had worked at more than eight different jobs, the longest lasting only six months. "If something doesn't turn up soon, I may enlist in the army," he said unenthusiastically.

"They'll probably draft you anyhow," Bunny consoled him.

"It's not likely, not while I'm still in school." He

must have seen her puzzled expression. "By the time I realized my mistake, I was too old to get back in regular school so I'm taking evening classes at Trade Tech."

Bunny stirred the ice in her glass. "I quit this summer. I had a good job at Paradine's. I'm expecting them to call me back any day." It was stretching the truth a little, but there was no harm in being optimistic.

"That's why you're haunting the employment office?" Tom probed.

Bunny flushed before that knowing look. She hadn't fooled him. "Okay, so they fired me," she admitted with a helpless grimace, "but I'm still on their list of relief workers. I can dream, can't I?"

To her relief, Tom dropped the subject of her unhappy relationship with Paradine's. "Funny, I never had you pegged for a dropout. It looks like we're both a couple of fools."

Bunny's straw stopped its revolving. She felt a prickle of annoyance. "What do you mean?"

"I mean being a dropout. How dumb can a person be?"

Bunny's annoyance mounted. "What's so great about school? I was just wasting my time. I may not have a job but I'll find one. Meanwhile, my experience at Paradine's did me a lot more good than nine months of ancient history or English literature—" She had not realized that her voice had risen.

"Hey, you don't have to get sore about it," Tom

protested. "I know how you feel. I felt the same way at first."

Bunny smiled apologetically. He really was nice. "I guess I'm just tired of everyone telling me what to do," she admitted.

He nodded. "You don't have to tell me what you're going through. I've been there and back."

When they finished their drinks, each left money on the counter. Tom lived on the east side of town with a married sister. "Maybe I'll see you next week," he said as they parted. He wasn't as lively as Dan or as polished as George, but he was a more comfortable person to be with. She hoped she would see him again.

Bunny overslept the next morning. Yesterday's sunlight had vanished behind a curtain of blustery clouds. Dressed in capris and a faded sweatshirt, she was doing the breakfast dishes when the telephone rang. Wiping her hands, she dashed for the other room, hoping it might be Paradine's. Instead, it was Mrs. Pierce. She had two job prospects: one, a finance company in the Centaur Building needed a file clerk; the other, a bookstore in the North Heights district wanted a saleswoman. Neither required previous experience. "You realize I have to give this information to another girl, too, but good luck to you," she said.

Bunny laid down the phone with trembling fingers. She had a choice of two jobs! This time she knew better than to dash off in a sweater and skirt. She dressed carefully in a tailored, dark blue dress, nylons and pumps. At eleven o'clock, the reflection of a neat, self-assured young woman smiled back at her from the mirror.

As the bus neared town, Bunny saw the tower of the Centaur Building ahead, but the sales job in the bookstore sounded more attractive. She transferred to the North Heights bus. She was not familiar with the neighborhood, and it was noon before she located the Cozy Corner Bookshop. The proprietor, a sprightly, rotund little man, would have resembled a jolly elf, except for his somber eyes.

"Do you love books, truly love them?" he asked in an intense voice.

The question caught Bunny unawares. "Why, I don't know. I guess they're all right," she stammered.

"Do you read a great deal?" he pursued.

"Not a whole lot," Bunny admitted honestly. Her face lit eagerly. "But I've had selling experience."

If possible, the little man's eyes grew more melancholy. He explained that he really wanted someone older, someone who kept up with the best sellers, was familiar with popular authors, enjoyed nonfiction and had some knowledge of children's literature.

Bunny left the store, anger temporarily eclipsing her disappointment. He had told Mrs. Pierce he would take someone inexperienced. What he really wanted was a walking encyclopedia! Why couldn't people say what they meant?

She returned to town and the Centaur Building. The manager of the Besco Finance Company had no trouble saying what he meant. "I'm sorry, you're too late. I filled that position an hour ago with another girl sent by the employment office."

Crestfallen, Bunny took the elevator back down to the foyer. If she had stopped at the Centaur Building first she probably would have gotten the job. Her resentment returned. It hardly seemed fair of Mrs. Pierce to send out more than one applicant for an opening. The sky overhead was still threatening. Feeling restless and unhappy, Bunny decided to walk. If it started to rain she could always duck under a store awning and wait for a bus.

As she headed south, the business district gave way to used car lots, garages and service stations, then scattered dwellings with an occasional neighborhood market or cluster of small businesses.

It was while she was waiting for a traffic light to change that Bunny saw the sign in the window of the Sprague Realty Company, in a diminutive yellow building that resembled an overgrown dollhouse. "Wanted—Girl Friday," it read.

She stared at it for almost a minute. They said the third time was the charm. She opened the door.

The room inside had only one occupant, a hearty-looking woman with a florid face and wiry ginger hair. "Yes, dear?" she questioned.

"I saw your sign in the window," Bunny replied. "I'm looking for a job."

If the office had seemed diminutive there was nothing small about the amazon who rose from behind the desk. Her smile was pleasant but unconvinced. "You look very young."

"I worked at Paradine's for six months," Bunny put in hastily. With a sickening feeling she realized that this was small qualification for a job in a real estate office. "I took some business courses in high school."

For the first time there was a spark of interest in the woman's eyes. "You can type?" she asked.

Earlier that morning at the bookstore Bunny had learned a bitter lesson about candid honesty. "I took typing," she admitted.

"How about shorthand?"

Bunny shook her head.

"Well, that isn't vital. I don't have much dictation," the woman said. "You have a pleasant voice, which is important." Bunny learned that she was Miss Sprague, the owner of the firm. For some time, she had managed with a part-time woman who came in mornings, but two weeks ago, the woman had quit; and now she was looking for a full-time assistant. The job would consist mainly of typing, filing and answering the telephone while she was out showing houses.

Bunny's heart galloped. "I'm sure I could handle it. It doesn't sound difficult."

"You're right. It isn't difficult work," Miss

Sprague agreed. "Actually, all I really require is typing. Why don't you just sit down at the machine over there and give me a sample of your work?"

Bunny's heart sank. It had been over a year since she had taken typing, and she was very rusty. Having come this far, there was nothing to do but brazen it through. Removing her gloves, she took her place at the smaller desk against the far wall. That clammy feeling had returned to her hands. As Miss Sprague handed her a letter to copy, the telephone rang.

"I have to rush over to the bank. Something about a signature on an escrow," Miss Sprague explained. Her large face brightened. "Why don't you type the letter while I'm gone? I won't be more than fifteen minutes."

As soon as Miss Sprague had disappeared, Bunny put a sheet of paper in the typewriter. She made a mistake and had to tear it out. She rolled in another sheet. Luck was with her; Miss Sprague was gone for a half hour. By going slowly and carefully, Bunny had a faultless letter laid on the desk when she returned. She even had time to empty the waste-paper baskets into the big barrel outside the rear door and straighten the magazine stand.

Miss Sprague was impressed with both the letter and her extra effort. "I like people who show initiative. There's no reason why I shouldn't at least give you a try." She explained that the salary would be fifty dollars a week, and Bunny could start the next morning.

Bunny left the office with an intoxicated feeling of success. So much for Tom Costa and his theories! She had found a job on her own again. A single, large raindrop hit her on the nose. It was hard to walk with sedate, ladylike steps when she wanted to pirouette. Another drop splashed on her nose. Discarding silly economy, she rode home in style in a taxi.

Even Mrs. Taylor was impressed by this job. "Real estate is a good field for women. You could learn a lot from this Miss Sprague. Later, you might even consider going to night school and taking some special courses."

Bunny's dreams that night were ecstatic ones. Dressed in a red wool dress with black fox trim exactly like one owned by Inez DeWitt, she was selling a well-dressed couple a building that looked like the Taj Mahal.

10

Calamity Jane

Promptly at eight thirty the next morning, Bunny was waiting outside the Sprague Realty Company. Her mind swirled with the last-minute advice thrust on her by her mother. *Do more than just what is required. Fill idle time usefully. Don't be afraid to use initiative.* Unfortunately, there was no way to put these into practice while waiting outside a locked office door for one's employer to arrive.

At five minutes to nine, Miss Sprague's blue sedan pulled to the curb. "I'm glad to see you have the virtue of promptness," she said. Once they were inside the small office, Bunny learned that she would not have to worry about displaying initiative immediately. Miss Sprague had been without an assistant for a week and had plenty of work to be done.

She gave Bunny two letters written in longhand. One was to be typed in triplicate. The other was a form letter to be sent to seven different homeowners who had recently put up For Sale signs, inviting them to list their property with Sprague Realty. "But before you start on those, I'd like you to answer this note from Mr. Jensen in Madera. Thank him for his interest but tell him I don't handle business property. However, I've given his name to someone who may be of assistance."

Before Bunny could nod that she understood, Miss Sprague was hurrying on. "Now I have an appointment this morning and will be gone until noon. While I'm away it will be up to you to answer the phone. Here's the appointment book and memo pad." She waved toward a stack of papers in a metal basket. "And when you finish, you can start filing those."

A little dazed, Bunny sat down at her desk. While Miss Sprague opened the mail, she peeked into the drawers. She noticed the desk had a thin layer of dust. When she had hung up her coat in the back room, she had seen a dust cloth. She got it and carefully dusted her desk and the other office furniture. "A splendid idea," Miss Sprague commended her. "A tidy office makes a good impression."

By the time Bunny had finished dusting, Miss Sprague had gone through the mail. She slipped her arms into her coat. With a hearty "Take care," she was gone.

Bunny sat alone at her desk, feeling important, awed and completely confused. Remembering that Miss Sprague had said to write to Mr. Jensen first, she rolled carbon and the paper into the machine. She typed his address and "Dear Sir." A sinking sensation filled her chest. They had written business letters in school, but that had been a long time ago.

She pushed back a wave of panic and yanked the sheet out of the machine. She would type the form letters first. That would get her started.

She made an error in the first paragraph and had to start over. The telephone rang. It was another realtor in North Heights who wanted to know if they had any listings on Park Terrace or Cheever. After a fruitless search of the files, Bunny returned to the phone. "I didn't find anything under Park Terrace, but there's a Frank Cheever on Thirtieth Street."

"No, no!" his voice exploded. "Not someone named Cheever—Cheever Street. You know, that winding dead end that overlooks the park. Multiple listing has nothing, but it's in your bailiwick and I thought Sprague might hold an exclusive—"

The conversation was meaningless gibberish to Bunny. She explained that she would have Miss Sprague return his call. "Yes, do that. She knows my number," he said curtly and hung up.

As Bunny reached for the memo pad, her pen

froze in midair. She hadn't gotten the realtor's name! He had mumbled it when he first called, but in all the running back and forth to the files it had slipped her mind. As she struggled to remember, she doodled a large M on the pad. Her spirits lifted. He had said he was from North Heights and Miss Sprague knew him, that should be identification.

The next time the phone rang, Bunny was careful to get the message straight. Between phone calls and making errors, she had only completed five of the form letters when Miss Sprague's car drew up in front. "Well, how did you get along?" she asked as she came through the door.

Bunny managed a wan smile. "All right, I guess. There were a lot of calls."

Miss Sprague nodded. "You look tired. Why don't you take your lunch hour now? I'll just sign the letters you have written and you can drop them in the box on the corner."

Bunny carried the letters to her desk. Miss Sprague looked at them incredulously. "You mean this is all you've done since nine this morning?"

Bunny nodded bleakly. "There were so many calls."

Miss Sprague's smile was fading. "But these form letters were the least important. I send out a hundred of these every year. The letter in triplicate has to be in the mail today." She took a deep breath. "You did write to Mr. Jensen?"

Bunny shook her head again.

"Good heavens, why not?" Miss Sprague's voice rose.

"I didn't know what to say," Bunny admitted.

Miss Sprague seemed to control herself with effort. Her voice was patient though strained. "I suppose it is hard, this being your first day. I don't wish to be unpleasant, but I'll have to ask you to put off going to lunch until you have written those letters. The Jensen letter doesn't require more than a couple of lines. I'll tell you what to say."

Bunny returned meekly to the typewriter. Miss Sprague picked up the memo pad. "What's this—M—North Heights?"

Bunny explained about the realtor who had called. "I didn't write down his name, but he said that he was from North Heights and you knew him."

"There are at least ten realtors in North Heights, and I know every one of them!" Miss Sprague cried. "M . . . M . . . I can't place who that would be."

Bunny's face turned crimson. "Oh, that doesn't stand for anything. I just put it down because he mumbled."

"Good heavens! Mr. Mumbles—now I've heard everything!" Miss Sprague's voice sounded faintly hysterical. "Don't you realize this bungling could cost me a commission? This afternoon I will have to telephone every single realtor in North Heights!"

Bunny seemed to be shrinking. "I'm sorry," she said in a small voice as she returned to her desk.

She took down in longhand the brief letter to Mr. Jensen. She had a splitting headache now. Aware that Miss Sprague was watching, she tried to make her typing brisk. She made several mistakes and had to erase them. Forty-five minutes had passed before she laid the letters on Miss Sprague's desk.

Miss Sprague frowned. "Just how much of a business course did you take in school?"

Even Bunny, standing at her shoulder, could see how smudged the letter looked with its erasures. "One year of business math and one of typing. I'm a little rusty. But with just a little practice, I'll improve."

With a sigh, Miss Sprague picked up the Jensen letter. "Oh merciful heavens! Erasures, smudges and now four simple words misspelled. This is too much!" To Bunny's horror, she crumpled the letter and threw it in the wastebasket.

Suddenly, for Bunny it was too much, too. Without a word, she plunged for the back room. She slammed the door of the washroom behind her. Leaning against it, she burst into tears. From almost the moment she had walked in this morning, it had been a day of horrors—a day of trying and failing, of one mistake mounting into another. At last, ashamed of her outburst, she splashed water on her puffy eyes and returned to the office.

Miss Sprague was retyping the letter to Mr. Jensen herself. No longer angry, she motioned for Bunny to be seated. "I'm sorry I lost my temper," she said, "but I am wondering if we aren't thinking the same thing?"

Bunny bobbed her head miserably. "I'm not going to work out, am I?"

"No, I'm afraid you aren't," Miss Sprague agreed. "I can't pay fifty dollars a week for someone to dust furniture while they learn typing. You simply do not have the experience for the job."

She paid Bunny five dollars for her morning's efforts and assured her that there was no need for her to stay on for the afternoon. "In one morning you have kept me from getting out two important letters and possibly cost me the sale of a Cheever Street house. I think that is sufficient *help* for one day."

Bunny did not find the remark as amusing as Miss Sprague seemed to think it was. She told herself if she had any pride she would refuse the money, but by now her pride had pretty well evaporated. Five dollars would pay for a lot of bus fares while she was looking for her next job.

She dreaded facing her family that night. Surprisingly, Doug had no comment at all, while her mother went out of her way to be sympathetic.

"Sounds to me like she was a bossy, demanding woman looking for experienced labor at slave wages," Mrs. Taylor defended with sudden, startling loyalty. She stopped frying hamburgers long enough to give Bunny a swift hug.

Bunny wished she hadn't. The sympathy made

her feel like crying again. Sometimes it was very difficult to be independent.

The following Monday morning, Tom was waiting beside the bulletin board at the employment office. When Bunny had picked up her check, he joined her at the door. "Over to the drugstore. It's banana splits this time."

"You got a job!" Bunny cried. She tried not to think of how just a few days ago she had been so sure that she would be the first with this news.

Tom waited until they were settled on the cracked leather stools and had given their orders to the man behind the counter, but his proud grin threatened to split his face. "You're right. This is my last shame money!" He waved his unemployment check. "I found the job myself. I've always been handy tinkering with cars, and they needed an apprentice at the Pacific Trucking Garage. The pay isn't much to start, but they're a big company with room for advancement."

"Oh, I'm so happy for you," Bunny cried, meaning every word. "When do you start work?"

"Wednesday," Tom replied. "In celebration, I used last week's unemployment check to fix up my car. So once I've stuffed you with bananas and whipped cream, I'll wheel you home in style."

Bunny laughed and dipped her spoon into the elaborate concoction that had just been set in front of her.

She did not refuse the ride. Later, as they headed down the boulevard in Tom's battered gray coupe, she remembered that flustered schoolgirl who had refused to let Dan drive her home from the park pool. She told herself that it was her new maturity in judging people, not loneliness, that had relaxed her standards. As they neared the Monterey Arms, she wished that the ride did not have to end so quickly.

Tom must have been thinking the same thing. "If you don't have anything else to do, why don't we drive on to the park? We can make faces at the animals in the zoo, or something."

"That sounds wonderful," Bunny agreed. "I'm chock full of resentments at the world. Except for the monkeys, they can't make faces back."

They parked across from the Youth Center and took the winding path that led toward the wire and cement enclosures of the small zoo. On week ends this area was crowded and noisy with families with small children; but today the graveled walks were almost deserted.

"You really are a big spender!" Bunny teased when Tom used a dime to buy peanuts for the monkeys.

"You haven't seen anything yet," he replied. "I'm not even going to wait for my first paycheck. I'm going to cash my unemployment check and invite you out to that dinner I promised, this Friday. That is, if you like Chinese food?"

"Love it," Bunny replied.

"Fine. It's the Bamboo Palace, then. If you eat

more than I can afford, I'll leave you behind to wash dishes."

"That could be the best job offer I've had all week," Bunny said with a laugh.

When the peanuts were gone, they found a place to relax on the grass. "All this talk about my job, how did things go for you this week?" Tom asked as he sprawled on his back.

Bunny bit a blade of grass and looked down into his square face. "Perfectly ghastly," she admitted.

She told him about the episode at the bookstore, the loan office and finally the miserable morning at the realty company. It was strange how things that had been so horrible at the time suddenly became humorous when shared with someone. "It really wasn't my awful typing that got me fired," she said. "I think it was Mr. Mumbles."

"Mr. *what*?" Tom asked.

"*M. M* for Mumble. I didn't catch his name, but I had to put something down, and he did mumble. Miss Sprague just didn't have any imagination."

Tom grinned. "Obviously a very dull woman."

Suddenly, both were laughing. "At least, I left the place cleaner than it was," Bunny said. "Whenever I get confused I always grab a dust rag and start flicking it around. It's a trick I picked up in housewares at Paradine's."

Tom chuckled. "I never learned the duster bit. That first year after I dropped out of school, my one defense was lying. I tried to make out like I was older than I was. Whenever I ran into some situation I couldn't handle, I'd try to squirm out of it with a lie. I was such a chump I lied my way out of three jobs in five months."

Bunny's eyes dropped into the grass. She remembered how she had tried to make Dan and George think she was older, those little lies she had told her mother, the lie to Mrs. Kurtz about the sunburst clock. She was glad when Tom dropped the subject.

For a moment, both were silent. "You know, you're a strange one," he said.

Bunny tossed her head and gave him a playful look. "Like I have three eyes maybe? Or a pickle growing on the end of my nose?"

He chuckled. "Like your eyes keep seeing the world the way you want it to be, not as it really is."

The afternoon with Tom had revived Bunny's enthusiasm. The next morning, when her mother and Doug had gone, she spread last night's newspaper on the kitchen table and returned to the want ads.

Her ardor decelerated as her eyes slid down the list. Beautician, dental technician, legal secretary, nurse—all took special training. A one-line ad near the bottom offered the only hope: "Telephone solicitors, no experience, Mrs. Adams 386-8881."

Bunny reached for the telephone. Mrs. Adams had a warm, vibrant voice, whose inflection im-

plied that they were close friends. She assured
Bunny that she had come to the right place. Their
solicitors worked from their own homes, and some
made as much as a hundred dollars a week. She
gave Bunny an address in the Riverview Building.
No appointment was necessary.

Dazzled, Bunny laid down the receiver. She had
learned her lesson about dawdling. Twenty minutes later, she was on her way into town.

The Riverview Building was located in an older
neighborhood of pawn shops, all-night restaurants
and encroaching warehouses. Bunny felt a moment's misgivings, but the directory by the elevator
revealed that along with numerous businesses, a
sprinkling of doctors, lawyers and professional
men also had offices in the building.

The Ever-Sell Company occupied a single room
on the fifth floor. One woman was seated behind a
desk near the door, while behind her in partitioned
cubicles three others talked on telephones. Mrs.
Adams had sounded like a huge, motherly woman.
Instead, she was small and thin-featured, with a
peculiar habit of pursing her lips at the conclusion
of each sentence. But the moment she started
talking, Bunny found herself hypnotized again by
that musical voice.

The Ever-Sell Company represented a variety of
clients. For Bunny, Mrs. Adams selected the Dandyware Company, which put out a complete line of
household products. She had nothing to sell but
was merely to make appointments with housewives

for a salesman to come out and demonstrate his wares. She was to mention that for every ten-dollar order, the purchaser was given her choice of an additional three-dollar item completely free. There was no obligation to buy. Even if the housewife purchased nothing, she still received a gift.

Bunny's face brightened. "You mean even if they don't buy anything, they still get the three-dollar gift?"

Mrs. Adams pursed her lips. "I hardly believe any company could be that extravagant. They'd be overwhelmed with people who had no intention of buying. But everyone gets something."

"What?" Bunny was curious.

"How should I know?" Mrs. Adams sounded annoyed. "I suppose it's some twenty-five- or fifty-cent item. All you need to say is '*a gift.*' " Bunny learned that she would receive one dollar for each firm appointment.

Riding home on the bus, she studied the Dandyware literature. At the very least, she should be able to make fifteen calls an hour. If just one out of five made an appointment, that would be three dollars an hour or twenty-four dollars a day!

Back home, she downed a hurried lunch, then she opened the telephone book to the A's. At the first two numbers, no one answered. The next found a man at home, but he hung up before she got started. It was not until the fourth call that she found someone who would listen. "Understand, there is no obligation to buy. All our salesman asks is that you allow him to show you our products, and he will leave you your gift," she ended breathlessly.

"Let me get this straight." The woman's voice was skeptical. "All I have to do is look at this stuff and I get a three-dollar gift?"

"Oh, no, the Dandyware Company couldn't afford that," Bunny explained honestly, "but they give you a smaller fifty-cent—"

There was a shrill laugh. "Good grief! For this you expect to waste my time!" Bunny stared unhappily at a phone that had gone dead again.

Mrs. Taylor did not think much of the job. She pointed out that the Ever-Sell Company had guaranteed nothing; moreover they were on a party line, and if Bunny held up the phone all day, there were going to be complaints. Bunny tried to hide her annoyance. That night she practiced her sales speech. If things went better the next day, she would put in her own private line.

Things did not go better. By noon her fingers were stiff from dialing, her voice hoarse from talking, and she had exactly one appointment. During the afternoon, she picked up another. Instead of twenty-four dollars, she had made two for a frustrating day's work.

As Bunny took the elevator to the fifth floor of the Riverview Building the following morning, she tried to think of some excuse to give Mrs. Adams. Unfortunately, there seemed to be none. "You mean these were all the appointments you were able to get? You certainly must not have spent much time!" Mrs. Adams said accusingly.

"But I did. I worked over eight hours," Bunny protested.

Mrs. Adams studied her thoughtfully. "You know, I believe you. Your trouble may be that you don't know how to make a sales talk."

A younger woman had stepped from one of the cubicles. She lit a cigarette and surveyed Bunny through a veil of blue smoke. "It's easy, kid. All you need is some gimmick."

"Give me that phone book," Mrs. Adams ordered. She selected a random number. "Mrs. Brenner? This is Mrs. Adams, right here in your neighborhood," she began in that warm, persuasive voice. "I sure hope I didn't catch you when you were busy? Fine. Because I want to tell you about the Dandyware Company. Honestly, they are the grandest folks, and guess what? They have just selected your name as one of those to receive a free gift. Now all you have to do is. . . ."

Bunny listened open-mouthed. She was quite sure that Mrs. Adams did not live in Mrs. Brenner's neighborhood. No one had selected Mrs. Brenner's name except Mrs. Adams herself! With a triumphant flourish, Mrs. Adams hung up and reached for an appointment slip.

"Like I said, you need a gimmick," the young woman repeated through another cloud of smoke. "That 'I live right in your neighborhood' bit goes over big with housewives. But I usually tell them we're running a contest. I make up a simple question, like, 'Who's the mayor of Bolton?' If they give the right answer, I tell them they've won a free gift. If they muff it I tell them the gift is the consolation prize."

Mrs. Adams nodded and surveyed Bunny with hungry eyes. "With your sweet, young voice you might do very well with a hard-luck story. You can say you're helping support your widowed mother and a crippled brother who needs an operation."

Bunny stared at the two of them with revulsion. Maybe she had told a few little falsehoods out of fear or confusion, but this was deliberate, calculated deceit. "But those are lies!"

Mrs. Adams laughed harshly. "Wake up, dearie, this is the twentieth century! We live in a competitive world. You tell the customers something they want to hear. You sell your client's product. Everyone is happy, so who's been hurt?"

Bunny felt sick inside. She still had a few ideals left. "Here's your book. I don't think I need your job after all," she blurted.

"With that attitude, it'll be a long time before you find another!" The young woman's jeering voice followed her through the door.

It wasn't until she was going down in the elevator that Bunny realized that she had forgotten to collect her two dollars. She told herself that she didn't want it. Nothing in the world would make her go back to that office and face greedy Mrs. Adams and that grinning smokestack again.

"There are plenty of legitimate telephone solicitors. You were just unlucky enough to run into a couple of chiselers," Tom consoled her as they were having dinner at the Bamboo Palace.

"I suppose so," Bunny admitted as she jabbed at a piece of bamboo shoot. "At least, I learned I haven't the personality for telephone selling. That's my trouble, I keep learning all the things I'm not cut out to be. I seem to be going at life backward."

"At our age, how many kids know what they want? The world isn't going to fall apart if we take our time deciding," Tom said.

"But every day we're getting older. I don't want to wake up when I'm eighty and discover that I really should have been a glass blower or a hippopotamus trainer," Bunny kidded.

Tom's mouth twisted into a grin. "I wouldn't panic yet. But if you're really worried, maybe you should arrange to take an aptitude test."

Bunny made a face. "I hate tests."

"This isn't the kind where you have to make a perfect score. It shows what your talents and interests are, and where you'd be the happiest."

Bunny shivered. "How could a test prove anything when I don't even know what kind of person I am myself? I'd be afraid I'd come out zero."

"You wouldn't," Tom assured her. "You may be a little mixed up, Bunny, but you're not any zero."

Bunny smiled. It was a left-handed compliment but nice. They had finished their chop suey, won ton and fried shrimp now. She broke open her fortune cookie. *"New friends and a happy change in your future,"* it said on the tiny slip of paper.

She glanced accusingly across the table at Tom. He had already eaten his cookie. "You didn't read your fortune."

"Yes, I did. They're silly. No one believes in them."

Bunny's eyes twinkled. "I do. I believe every word."

It was the first time she had ever seen Tom look embarrassed. He handed her the ribbon of crumpled paper. She smoothed it open carefully: *"The one you have been waiting for has already come into your life."*

She could feel Tom watching her intently. She was not sure yet that she wanted to be the one he was waiting for. "You're right, I guess they are silly," she told him with a quick grin, but she kept the slip of paper and put it in her purse.

11

The River Rats

There ought to be a law against being lonely in the spring, Bunny thought as she washed the breakfast dishes. Beyond the windows the plane trees looked like a French impressionist painting with their splashes of yellow-green and pale blue shadows. A gardener somewhere nearby had finished mowing a lawn, and the breeze stirring the curtains mingled the distant musky smell of the river with the closer, more intimate odor of new-mown grass. It was a golden day filled with promise, only with no one to share it, the promise was like an empty husk.

Bunny thought of Tom, who probably was at work by now. Next Saturday, he had asked her to go to a show, and Sunday he had mentioned a picnic at the park; but she rather resented the night school classes that kept her from seeing him all week. Unless she found a job soon, she would become another Mary Benson, living from week end to week end.

Fortunately, it was Monday and the day of her weekly visit to the employment office. Afterward, she told herself, she might walk over to see Sandy and the new baby, who were home from the hospital.

Because there was no reason to hurry, she was later than usual in arriving at the employment office. Today, the paprika-haired girl fell in behind her. Bunny was no longer surprised when she had no call for an interview. Apparently they did not have any prospects for the other girl either. She caught up with Bunny halfway across the room. "From the way old Beetlebrows glowers, you'd think he was paying us out of his own pockets."

"From the size of my check, he wouldn't miss much," Bunny replied. The girl laughed, sympathetically. Today, she had left her companion standing by the door. He joined them. Aside from the fact that he needed a haircut, he was rather good-looking, with a natural wave in his sunbleached hair, quizzical eyebrows and bold gray eyes.

"Where's your boy friend today?" the girl asked.

Bunny was puzzled until she realized that she was talking about Tom. "He got a job," she answered.

"Lucky him," the boy said.

"Oh, he found it all by himself," Bunny explained.

He grimaced. "That figures. As you've probably noticed we're the unmentionables around here."

"We've seen you around before. My name's Beverly Gibson but you can call me Bev." The girl nodded toward her companion. "He's Jonathan Wallace, better known as Jock."

"Hi," Bunny said. "I'm Benecia Taylor, only everyone calls me Bunny."

For no reason at all, everyone laughed. It was crazy the way parents struggled to pick out fancy names when they should have known they'd be changed.

"How about joining us at the drugstore for a Coke?" Bev invited. "Only it'll have to be Dutch. Until we cash my check, we're flat busted except for twenty cents."

"Dutch is fine with me," Bunny agreed. "I'm loaded. Counting pennies, I think I have eighteen cents."

They burst into laughter again. "Imagine meeting an heiress!" Jock hooked his other arm through hers.

By the time she had settled on the worn leather stool, Bunny had decided that she liked them. They were young, they could laugh and they were friendly. Right now, she couldn't think of three more endearing qualities.

"How long have you been out of work?" she asked Jock.

"All my life," he replied wearily.

"He exaggerates," Bev said. "He's eighteen years and seven months old and he has only been unemployed eighteen years and two months. He's not like Fink, who is twenty and has been unemployed every year, month and day of his wasted life."

"Fink is our friend," Jock said as though some explanation was necessary. "Actually once when he was eight a man offered him a quarter to take a letter to the post office, but he refused. Even as a child he recognized his destiny."

Bunny suppressed a giggle. They were out of work, but they still could joke.

In a more serious vein, Bev explained that Jock had drawn his last unemployment check three weeks ago. Her own compensation only had one more payment to go.

"You mean in all this time the employment office hasn't found either of you a job?" Bunny asked.

"Listen to the naïve child!" Jock hooted. "She still believes in Santa. We are dropouts, Bev and I —spelled *d-r-o-p-o-u-t*. Just to be a teen-ager is to have some kind of disease. To be a teen-age dropout is to have it in the worst form. Don't you read the papers? We are the unemployable. One authority says not to give us jobs to force us back to school. The Job Corps says to give us jobs to keep us off the streets. Everyone else closes his eyes and wishes we'd quietly disappear."

Bunny was a little startled by the tirade until

Bev winked. "Don't mind him, he sounds off all the time."

Bunny grinned. She realized from the hidden laughter in their eyes that Jock was half-teasing, but a lot of what he said was true. The fact that both Bev and Jock were dropouts made them seem closer. She learned that Jock had left school two years ago, Bev, just this fall like herself. Their straws made scraping noises on the bottoms of their glasses.

"I don't have much gas in my car, but if you aren't going too far we'll give you a lift," Jock offered.

There was a catch in Bunny's throat at the thought of parting. She shook her head. "Thanks, but I live down by Memorial Park. Walking gives me something to do."

"You mean you just hang around home all day?" Bev exchanged looks with Jock. "Why don't you come along to the river with us? We're on our way down to the marina."

Bunny's heart quickened. "You're sure I wouldn't be in the way?" she asked, aware that they were a twosome.

"Of course not," Jock replied. "You don't need a formal invitation to join the River Rats. Bev has to be home by four o'clock, I'll see that you get a ride back at the same time."

"You'll need warmer clothes, though," Bev said, as though everything was settled. Minutes later, they were heading down Park Boulevard in a black convertible with a ragged top.

Bev and Jock waited in the car while Bunny dashed into the apartment and changed into slacks and a sweater. "Who are the River Rats?" she asked as she tumbled into the car again. As they roared away from the curb, she realized it was a question she should have asked much earlier.

"You—us—everyone," Jock answered with a vague wave of his hand.

It was Bev who put her at ease. "It isn't a club or anything, just the nickname we give the crowd that hangs out down at the marina. It's a good spot. We don't bother anyone. The boys pick up odd jobs working around the boats. In winter, when things are dead, Skiff lets us hang around his café because it makes the place look busy."

Because they lived so close to Memorial Park with its many facilities, Bunny had only driven past the smaller Marina Park once in Midge Willoughby's car. Actually it wasn't much of a park, just a narrow strip of grass and trees that stretched for a quarter of a mile along the river. At the lower end, where there were a few battered picnic tables, one saw a scattering of fishermen in midsummer. Farther up, was a small roped-off area for swimming. At the north end, immediately adjoining the grounds and private anchorage of the Yacht Club, was a promenade lined with refreshment stands and the floating docks of the city-owned marina.

As Jock stopped the car in the parking lot,

Bunny saw that most of the boats were bedded down in brown canvas for the winter, and the refreshment stands were boarded closed except for one small café on a pier, called Skiff's. In warm weather, the customers could eat outside overlooking the river, but today the chairs were stacked upside-down on the tables. Even inside, the café seemed deserted, except for a single fisherman eating at one of the booths and two boys dressed in jeans and sweatshirts at the end of the counter.

A big, red-faced man glanced from his stool behind the counter with disinterested eyes. "Hello, anybody buying?"

"Just sitting, Skiff," Jock replied easily. "Unless you'd like to extend us some of your well-known credit."

"Well-known, my clavicle!" the big man snorted good-naturedly. "Warm the stools, *si*. Credit, no. Only remember, I don't expect you to sit there all day. If some paying prospects come in, you shove."

"Yes, sahib." Bev bobbed her head mockingly.

The two boys at the end of the counter had lifted their hands in a friendly salute. Bev introduced the tall muscular one as Tor; his short dark-haired companion was Blackie. Tor was working on one of the yachts at the marina that day. Blackie, who had picked up a few dollars earlier in the morning at the Yacht Club, was hanging around watching him.

"Where's Fink?" Jock asked.

"Last I knew he was laying out at the end of the float trying to catch a fish," Tor replied.

"A fish? What would Fink want with a fish?" Bev cried.

"You know Fink!" Blackie made a circular motion near his ear. "Greta went out to make sure he hadn't gone to sleep and fallen in."

Moments later, the door was opened by a short plump girl with freckles, who was leading a thin black-haired boy by the hand. The boy wore lashed-off khaki-colored pants, a faded pink T-shirt, and in spite of his youthful face, sported a curly, black beard. "Greta and Fink." Bev made more introductions. "In case you haven't guessed, Fink is a professional hair grower."

"Blasphemy," Fink muttered, but his large, dark eyes were friendly.

"Oh, quit glowering," Tor told Skiff. "You'll make the mortgage payment today." He dug some money out of his pocket and dropped it on the counter. He did not ask what anyone wanted. Skiff brought everyone a Coke. Before Bunny could thank him, Tor had crossed the room, put a dime in the record player and asked Bev to dance. Jock was talking to Blackie. Fink touched Bunny's arm. "Afraid to dance with a bearded man?"

She slid from the stool. "I think you look very distinguished."

"Please don't say that," he complained. "It thwarts my purpose in life."

"What is your purpose?" she asked.

148

"Being nothing," he told her solemnly. "My life is devoted to being absolutely nothing—nameless, worthless, a nonentity. I have a theory that once I achieve the ultimate, I'll become invisible."

Bunny was startled until she caught that hidden twinkle in his eyes. He was crazy but in a gentle, zany sort of way. To her surprise, he was an excellent dancer. The only trouble was that he was barefoot, and she kept worrying that she would step on his toes.

After having paid for their Cokes and danced one dance with Bev, Tor disappeared. Jock explained that he had returned to his job. For an hour, they had fun talking and dancing. Finally they wandered out to the dock and found Tor, who was scrubbing the deck of a white boat. They sat cross-legged on the floating dock and talked to him while Greta passed around a bag of potato chips. Fink, sprawled on his stomach, was fishing again with a hand line dropped over the edge. When Blackie reached under the dock with a long gaff and made Fink's line bob up and down as though he had a bite, everyone roared with laughter.

Some of them drifted back to Skiff's, but Jock had fallen asleep, sprawled in the sun. Bunny remained behind, too, enjoying the warm sunlight on her back and watching to see if Fink caught anything. At last, Tor had finished. He leaped noisily from the boat, waking Jock. Fink pulled in his line, and the four of them walked back to the café. To Bunny's dismay, it was empty.

"Where's Bev?" she gasped.

Jock shrugged. "She probably went home with Greta and Blackie. Don't worry, I'll take you home."

"It isn't that—" Bunny stammered. "I thought Bev was your girl."

Jock laughed. "We don't have girl friends. We're too darn poor to afford them. We're all just pals."

Bunny still wished that Bev hadn't disappeared, but there was nothing she could do about it. Tor had his own car, but Jock offered Fink a ride home, too. Fink lived north of town in a district of surprisingly elegant homes. They dropped him on a corner and turned back. They had gone only a few blocks when the car's motor gave a couple of dyspeptic coughs and died.

"What's wrong?" Bunny asked worriedly.

"Out of gas," Jock explained, "and just my luck I don't have a dime!"

Bunny opened her purse. All she had was eight cents. She looked worriedly at her watch. It was almost five. It had taken longer than she had expected to drive Fink home. She should have left a note for her mother. "All I have is my unemployment check," she said.

"Well, what are we waiting for? Let's cash it." Jock was already climbing from the car. Bunny followed him, aware of a vague, uneasy feeling.

They had to walk five blocks to find a service station where they could cash her check. "Might as well make it five gallons," Jock directed. "I'll carry one back to the car and drive in for the rest."

Bunny was unusually silent as they drove home. "Be seeing you," Jock called lightly as he let her off in front of the apartment house.

To Bunny's relief, she was ahead of her mother. As she climbed the stairs, she wished that uneasy feeling would go away. She had enjoyed every minute of the afternoon, but there was something about the River Rats that bothered her. She wished Jock hadn't roared off without even asking for her phone number or mentioning that he would pay her back for the gas. Could it be that he and Bev had just picked her up because they thought she had some money?

12

If the Name Fits . . .

The following morning, Bunny awoke again to that lonely, restless feeling. As she ate breakfast, she tried not to think of Bev and Jock. It seemed unlikely she would ever see them again. At nine o'clock, she had settled down to go through yesterday's want ads when she heard an auto horn outside. It continued rhythmic and insistent.

Curiosity drove her to the window. The honking had stopped, and a tall boy with unkempt blond hair and a slender, red-haired girl were getting out of a black convertible. It was Jock and Bev!

Bunny flung open the window and shouted.

"We were about to start ringing doorbells," Bev

yelled back. "We couldn't remember your last name so we didn't know which apartment to try. Are you busy today?"

Bunny only heard the last sentence. She shook her head vigorously.

"Come along with us to the river," Jock invited. He dug into his pocket, and there was a flash of green in the sunlight. "I've got your money for you."

Bunny ducked her head back inside. It took only seconds to wiggle into a warm sweater. "I don't know if anyone will be around this early, but it's something to do," Bev said as she tumbled into the car beside them.

Bunny had to agree. Maybe it was only nine in the morning, but it was wonderful to be heading somewhere, knowing you had something to do for the day. How she had misjudged them!

They found the café on the pier deserted, though Skiff said that Tor and Blackie had been in earlier. They talked and waited. When Skiff began to glower at them for hanging around so long, Bev bought a sweet roll for everyone and Bunny put a dime in the record player. Finally, Jock suggested that they walk over to the Yacht Club and look for Blackie.

A sign on the entrance said "Private—Members Only"; but it was obvious that Bev and Jock had been there before. They did not follow the drive as far as the clubhouse, a long, white building with tinted glass windows. At the parking lot they took some cement steps that led directly to the docks. They found Blackie working on a cabin cruiser. When he saw them he called to someone in the cabin. Greta's head popped out. "The way they've been patrolling this place, I've been keeping out of sight," she explained.

She joined them on the dock. The boats here seemed larger and more elegant than those at the city marina. While Jock talked to Blackie, the girls wandered about admiring some of the more expensive yachts. Ten minutes later, Bunny discovered why Greta had been keeping out of sight. A man in a blue-gray uniform came hurrying along the dock. He explained politely but firmly that they would have to leave since they were not members of the club or working for anyone who was.

No one protested. Waving to Blackie, they started back the way they had come. "What a bunch of stuffed shirts," Greta complained. "Hiring a guard is something new. Until last month they never minded as long as we stayed away from the clubhouse."

"I can't see what difference it makes. We were just talking to Blackie," Bunny agreed.

Bev rolled her eyes. "Oh, you know how people are about teen-agers. They're sure we're going to steal something."

"Why, that's silly!" Bunny's voice was indignant.

Beside her Greta had started to giggle. Jock had

slid something from under his sweater. It was a white yachting cap. He popped it on his head at a rakish angle and grinned at them.

"Where did you get that?" Bunny gasped.

He shrugged. "I found it. Now I've got the hat, all I need is for one of you girls to buy me a yacht." He waved his arms expansively.

Everybody burst into laughter except Bunny. "Shouldn't you take it back?" she asked.

"Back where?" Jock teased. "The rich slobs who own those boats buy these caps by the dozen. Someone probably threw this one away."

Bunny had to admit the cap appeared well worn. She decided Jock was right. Besides, it made him look very handsome.

They had almost reached the marina when they saw a white motorboat turning in toward the dock. The tall, jean-clad figure behind the wheel raised his arm. It was Tor. Jock raced down to help him tie up.

Tor explained that he had been giving the boat's motor a trial, because its owner was taking out a fishing party on Saturday. "I've got to tinker with her a little more, but stick around and I'll give you a ride."

They went back to Skiff's for hamburgers. Greta didn't have any money, but everyone chipped in enough to buy her lunch. She did her share by furnishing the music. She set her small transistor radio on the counter where everyone could hear.

When Skiff got mad because she was playing it too loud, they moved to one of the outside tables. Bunny was beginning to understand their casual attitude toward money. They were completely democratic. What one had he shared with the others. It created an even closer feeling of camaraderie.

At one thirty, Tor was ready to test the boat's motor. He and Jock helped the girls aboard. "Are you sure this is all right?" Bunny asked worriedly.

Tor laughed. "It doesn't take any more gas for five than it does for one. Besides, you can tell me how the motor sounds."

Bev giggled. "I can tell you already. It goes putt-putt-putta."

"No, there's something wrong." Jock pushed back his yachting cap and assumed a serious air. "It's quite simple. The thingamagizzle isn't getting enough rachet oil into the culpepper nut so that the carmoxies aren't puffulated."

Everyone including Bunny burst into laughter. She leaned back against the leather seat enjoying the rush of brisk air against her cheeks and the musky odor of the river. They went several miles down the river, then because the motor was sounding all right, they turned back. It had been such fun she wished that the ride could have lasted longer.

Bunny was home by three o'clock that afternoon and had dinner waiting for her mother. When she heard about Bunny's day, Mrs. Taylor's forehead puckered. "Hanging around the waterfront doesn't sound like any place for teen-agers. Why aren't those young people working?"

"It isn't the waterfront, it's the yacht harbor," Bunny corrected sharply. "All of them are looking for work just like me. It's not their fault they haven't found anything."

She was glad when her mother did not argue the point, but it seemed unfair to condemn her new friends without even having met them.

The following day Mrs. Pierce called and Bunny went downtown for a job interview. As happened so often, they wanted someone older, but as she left the office Bunny did not feel the usual depressing sense of failure. The River Rats had done that much for her. It made it easier when you knew there were others in the same boat.

Friday, she returned to the river for another lazy afternoon with Bev and Jock. On Sunday, Blackie was borrowing a boat and had invited everyone for a cruise on the river. "Well, you don't have to sound so enthused!" Bev teased Bunny, who had become rather quiet.

When Bunny explained that she already had a date with Tom, they insisted that she bring him along, too. "You're sure you wouldn't mind?" she asked.

Jock laughed. "Why should we? Just because he was lucky enough to land a job doesn't mean he's some kind of monster."

"You're going to like them," Bunny told Tom confidently as they headed toward the marina on Sunday morning.

His dark eyes were teasing. "You mean they'll give me rosy cheeks, too. I don't think I could stand being that beautiful!"

Bunny laughed. Tom had teased her about her sunburn last night when he had taken her to the show. "Silly, I mean they're all dropouts, too." Tom gave her a sharp look. "You call that a recommendation?"

Bunny bit her lip and stared out the window. For the first time, she wondered if she had done the right thing by bringing Tom along. He was nice, but if he got off on all that talk about night school and getting a diploma, she didn't think he would go over very well.

She need not have worried. The River Rats accepted Tom as easily as they had her. Instead of gathering at Skiff's, they had assembled on the promenade. Jock explained that Skiff was temporarily mad at them. Two nights before someone had broken into his cigarette machine and stolen all the money. "You know how it is. If there's a teen-ager within ten miles, he's guilty."

Tom nodded. "Tell me no tales. Yesterday someone goofed on a repair job at the garage and you know who almost got fired before the boss found out the truth."

Fink patted his shoulder. "This lad, corrupted as

he is by the filthy world of the employed, is one of
us."

"When did you leave school?" Jock asked Tom.

"On my sixteenth birthday, naturally; doesn't
everyone?" Tom replied. Bunny let out her breath.
She was glad he had not mentioned night school.

Jock explained that Blackie preferred to pick
them up in the marina. It looked better than
having them come to the Yacht Club. At last, they
saw the brown and white cruiser slicing across the
strip of water that separated them from the club
anchorage. It took only seconds for everyone to
scramble aboard, then with a thrust of its big
motor, the cruiser was shooting out into the river.
The wind whipped Bunny's hair back from her
face as she and Tom found a seat on the canvas
cushions. Bev and Jock crowded in beside them.
Greta and a new boy named Hutch stretched out
on the top of the cabin in the sun. Only Fink and
Tor seemed restless. "I thought you were bringing
water skis," Tor said.

"Wait until we get farther down the river. There
are too many people around here," Blackie replied.

With a shrug, Tor sat down. Occasionally, they
passed another boat, but it was still early in the
year for many people to be on the river. They no
longer saw the roofs of warehouses and sprouting
TV antennas above the walls of the levees but just
a distant barn or farmhouse.

"I've got to get some fuel before we do much
racing around," Blackie said.

"Why didn't you get it at the Yacht Club?" Jock asked.

"Because Mr. Petersen always deals with Petros across the river, and I can charge it there," Blackie replied.

Minutes later, Bev pointed toward some red-roofed buildings. "Hey, isn't that Petros?"

"I know, I know," Blackie said without turning. "I'll take you down to the picnic spot first, then come back for it."

"But that's out of your way," she protested.

"Do I have to explain everything? I can't go into Petros to fill up with this gang aboard," Blackie snapped. He must have seen the question in their eyes. "Look, Mr. Petersen doesn't mind if I use the boat. I know he wouldn't mind my bringing you along. But he's back in Denver this week; there was no way I could ask. So why make waves?"

Bunny joined the others in nodding agreement. She noticed Tom did not say anything. Several miles down the river, Blackie swung the cruiser toward shore and what looked like the burned ruins of an old landing. The pier was half-submerged, but with the boys' help the girls were able to make their way to the bank, where they found sheltering trees, a sandy beach and plenty of firewood.

Though the last week had been sunny, the water still looked too cold to Bunny for swimming. She was content to lounge on the beach, but when Blackie returned some of the others took turns water skiing. Later, they were joined by three other couples, but when they got hungry the fellows pooled their money and someone drove inland to a little rural store to buy the things for a weenie bake.

It was a lazy, happy day. By the time Blackie dropped them off at the marina dock that evening, its lights and those from the Yacht Club stretched like wavery, yellow fingers across the water.

In the parking lot, Bunny said good night to the others. "See you later, Tom," several called with friendly voices.

"Well, what do you think of them?" Bunny asked once they were in Tom's car.

"You want the truth?" he asked.

It wasn't the answer that she had expected. "Of course, I want the truth," she replied in a puzzled voice.

"I think their name fits," Tom said grimly.

"I don't understand," Bunny stammered.

"River Rats—it fits," Tom repeated. "Bunny, I don't know how you ever got in with this outfit, but they're nothing but a bunch of bums."

Bunny turned in shocked surprise. "How can you say that after the wonderful way they treated you, inviting you for a free boatride and picnic, asking you to come back?"

"I can say it, because I've seen their kind before. You know as well as I do, they were using that boat without the owner's permission."

"You heard what Blackie said. Mr. Petersen doesn't care."

"You heard what you'd like to believe. That's what you really heard. Grow up, Bunny, these kids spell one thing, and that's trouble."

"Oh, sure, just because you have a job you can be high and mighty," she cried. "The fact that they're still looking for work makes them bums."

"A lot of looking most of them are doing!" Tom scoffed. "Fink, Greta and Hutch have never worked a day in their lives. Jock worked five months, drew what unemployment checks he could, and now he's a loafer, too. Tor and Blackie are content with the petty change they pick up around the boats; they aren't looking for anything steady."

"If they aren't looking it's only because they've discovered it's a useless search! Everyone's against them."

"I don't suppose they ever heard of the Job Corps," Tom snapped.

Bunny sniffed. "Jock says all they do is send you off to pick onions or something."

"Boy, they really have you brainwashed!" Tom replied.

Bunny thought of Fink, with his big, gentle eyes; Jock, with his bravado when things went wrong; Bev, who practically loved the whole world. Sitting there staring straight ahead with his mouth set grimly, Tom looked stuffy, pompous and opinionated. She wondered how she ever could have liked him. "Are you through criticizing my friends, or would you like to let me out here?" she asked coldly.

Tom did not say another word until they had reached the apartment. He reached across her and opened the door. "If you wake up one of these days and need a friend, I'm in the phone book," he said gruffly.

"Thanks, I wake up needing a case of poison ivy all the time!" Bunny slammed the door and ran up the walk.

13

Run, Thief, Run!

"Did you hear about the new law they're thinking of passing?" Blackie asked.

Bev stifled a yawn. "No, tell us."

"They're going to make it a crime to be young. Only they can't figure out the punishment: imprisonment until you get your first gray hair, or twenty-five years banishment to Outer Oblivion."

"You sound like Jock. What brought this on?" Bev asked.

"That cop stopping us last night for no reason at all, that's what," Blackie said. "Here Tor and I are driving along minding our own business when this boy on the bicycle motions us over to the curb, makes us get out and goes over the car like maybe we've got a Roosian spy in the trunk. When he doesn't find anything, does he apologize? Not him.

'Behave yourselves,' he says. Behave yourselves;" Blackie repeated in a mocking falsetto.

"We're juvenile delinquents, didn't you know?" Bev replied. "Everyone too young to vote and too old for roller skates is a juvenile delinquent. You ought to read the newspapers."

"Who can read?" Blackie grunted.

Bunny smiled and rolled over to let the sun tan the front of her legs. It was April, with warming days that already hinted at summer. The trees were green canopies overhead; in the gardens azaleas dripped with blossoms, and on week ends the river was striped with the white wakes of small boats. There had been little time to miss Tom; the River Rats had seen to that.

Good weather had brought the do-it-yourself yachtsmen out of hibernation to work on their boats, and it was getting harder for the boys to find odd jobs. They accepted the change philosophically. Today, all were sunning themselves on the park lawn opposite the dock.

"Dame Fortune always provides," Jock announced with a grin as he returned from Skiff's carrying a couple of packs of cigarettes. "This week's special—two for the price of one."

Tor deftly caught the extra pack. "Man, that's twice now! If you don't watch out, you'll be as sharp as Fink."

At the sound of his name, Fink opened one brown eye. He sat up and acknowledged the compliment with a bow. Then he lay back, closed his eyes and pretended to be snoring. Bunny joined in the laughter. While it was quite a trick to persuade a cigarette machine to give up two packs for the price of one, Fink was recognized as the master. Armed with only a bobby pin or wad of tin foil, he could place telephone calls, get a free hour on the parking meter or persuade a candy machine to cough up a half dozen bars for a single nickel. If some small voice whispered to Bunny that these things were dishonest, she muffled it with the thought that she never actually did them herself.

It was a lazy, placid life. Bunny could not go to the river every day, but she managed a ride with Jock or one of the others three or four times a week. By now her unemployment checks had stopped, but she had taken a babysitting job two nights a week with a young couple in one of the apartments downstairs. It furnished what spending money she needed. With the River Rats, there was no need for pretense. With them, it did not matter that she did not have a job or money or had not finished school.

"How do you know that Paradine's or Mrs. Pierce have not called. You're never here to answer the phone," Mrs. Taylor complained angrily one evening. "I know Paradine's have had at least three big sales since they let you go. If you weren't so stubborn, you'd do as I suggest and phone to make sure you're still on their relief list."

Bunny stifled an angry reply. If it meant that she never worked again, she wouldn't go begging back to Paradine's. As for the employment office, she'd already seen how much help they were! It seemed to her that she and her mother bickered constantly now. Mrs. Taylor did not approve of the time she spent at the marina. Bunny thought this was unfair, since she always got home in time to fix dinner. And she hardly ever went out with her new friends in the evening. Actually, there wasn't much to do after dark. It was too cold to go to the river, and they seldom had money for a show. Mostly, the fellows cruised around by themselves or hung out at Beasley's, a drive-in on the north side where some of the high school crowd went in the evenings.

One sunny morning in mid-April, Jock and Bev didn't turn up at ten o'clock as they had promised. By now, Bunny had Bev's telephone number, but when she called the house no one answered. After lunch, she was settling down for a lonely afternoon watching television when she heard the familiar beep outside. Jock was alone. As Bunny slid in beside him, her heart skidded. His face looked strained and pale.

"Is something wrong?" she asked.

"Is there!" He nodded grimly. "They caught Fink last night, fooling around with a candy machine down on River Street."

"How awful!" Bunny gasped in shocked surprise. She relaxed a little. "But that really isn't such a terrible crime."

"It's against the law, that's enough," Jock replied. "Besides, he had a load of dimes in his pockets that looked like they'd come from some coin box, and I heard they're trying to tie his fingerprints in with that cigarette-machine job at Skiff's last month. The crazy nut. Shaking a machine for a little extra loot is one thing, but I told him to leave those coin boxes alone. They really have him now."

Bunny felt a little sick as she thought of Fink with his stubbed bare toes, ragged pants and gentle, puppy-dog eyes.

"That's the reason I was so late," Jock continued. "Bev's already gone down to the marina with Greta and Blackie. I've been around contacting everyone to make sure we all have our story straight."

"What do you mean?" Bunny was puzzled.

"Why, about Fink, natch. If some cop comes around asking questions we all want to say the same thing. As far as we know Fink was a loner, a real oddball. He hung around the marina, but none of us had anything to do with him."

Bunny's mouth dropped. "But that's not true. Fink was our friend!"

"Look, we can't help Fink any by getting involved in this," Jock explained. "Later, if he goes to jail, we can write or send him things. Right now, we're better off keeping out of it. Remember, if anyone asks—you hardly knew him. You thought he was a dope, a real drip. Got it?"

"Yes, I got it," Bunny said in a small, cold voice.

She did not enjoy herself much that afternoon. The river was dazzling under a bright sun, eight of the gang were gathered around one of the outdoor tables at Skiff's, but as she sipped her soft drink, Bunny kept thinking of Fink sitting in a jail somewhere. She remembered how he used to wander off from the others to sit on the end of the dock, fishing. She had never seen him catch anything, but sometimes she had joined him, just enjoying sitting in the warm sun and thinking her own thoughts.

Leaving the others, she wandered out on the dock and sat down cross-legged at the end, staring across the muddy, moving water. She wondered if they'd make Fink shave his beard. She wouldn't recognize him without it. She hoped they would send him to one of those honor camps out in the country; he liked it outdoors.

She heard footsteps. Bev had followed her. "What's eating you? Wandering off by yourself, you're liable to become as kookie as Fink," she complained.

Bunny didn't answer, just shrugged. To her surprise, Bev sank down beside her. "After awhile even this gets to be a rat race," she commented bitterly. "I'm thinking of cutting out."

Bunny looked at her in surprise.

As though embarrassed, Bev studied her painted toenails. "I've got a married sister down in San

Francisco. She's asked me to come live with her. A couple of blocks from her place is a beauty college. If I'm a good kid and baby-sit with her brats in the evening, she and her husband will stake me to a course at the school."

Bunny nodded. "That sounds pretty good."

"Good, bad, who really cares? I can't hang around here sponging off my folks forever," Bev said.

Bunny never saw Bev again. When she didn't show up at the river, someone said that she had moved to San Francisco. No one seemed to miss her. The crowd was like that, new members attached themselves to the group, old ones wandered away.

The following Thursday, Bunny was seated in Skiff's, eating a hamburger, when she noticed a thin, brown-haired boy studying her dubiously from the doorway. "Can you help me? I'm looking for someone named Jock," he said.

Bunny started to nod toward the record player, but Jock was already returning. "Hi," he said curiously.

"Are you Jock?" the boy asked.

Jock shrugged. "I might be and I might not. Why?"

"The gang over at Beasley's said you might be able to fix me up with a radio."

Jock made a motion with his head. "Come on outside," he said.

Blackie took the vacant stool beside Bunny. "You look deserted," he teased.

"I am," she replied. "Jock's outside with someone who wants to buy a radio."

Blackie's forehead puckered. "What's going on?" he asked when Jock returned.

"Some kid, looking for a radio. He's got twenty dollars. Know anyone with a twenty-dollar radio for our friend?"

Blackie grinned. "Do I? That's just the price this guy is asking, too."

There was something about their laughter that made Bunny uneasy. Finishing her hamburger, she wandered outside. Greta was talking to Tor, who was bailing one of the small rowboats that Skiff had for hire.

"Hello, beautiful, how about giving me a hand?" he greeted her. Bunny accepted a mouthful of popcorn from Greta's bag, then seized a can and began scooping water. It was more fun out here in the warm sunlight. Whatever Jock and Blackie were planning, she told herself that it was none of her business.

That night Bunny had to baby-sit for the couple downstairs, but Friday Jock suggested casually that they all get together for a show. It was Bunny's first evening date in several weeks, but she still saw those tightening lines around her mother's lips. "Be home early," she warned.

Something about the unwarranted disapproval stirred a rebellious feeling in Bunny's chest. She fidgeted restlessly, wishing her friends would hurry.

As soon as she got into Jock's convertible and saw Blackie lounging alone in the back, Bunny knew the show was out. "Maybe next week, Greta couldn't get away tonight," Jock explained. "I thought we'd run down to Skiff's. Blackie wants to see someone."

Bunny tried to conceal her disappointment. She had gotten dressed up for nothing. At the corner, Jock pulled up beside a carload of teen-agers and revved his motor with a rumbling challenge. Though the convertible was old, the engine was in top condition. It was no race; they pulled away from the competition with a spiteful roar. The night was balmy and the street and store lights flashing past the car window blurred into a colored ribbon of excitement. By the time they pulled into the parking lot, Bunny's spirits had revived.

Cars were turning into the entrance of the Yacht Club, and the clubhouse lights were ablaze. At the marina it was more peaceful. The reflected lights of the pier floated like golden water lilies in the dark water, and the gentle tug of the current made musical lapping noises against the pilings.

They parted with Blackie in the parking lot. "We'll wait for you at Skiff's," Jock said.

There were a few people at the restaurant: several couples drinking coffee, a group of fishermen having a late dinner. They sat at the counter and ordered Cokes and french fries. "Where are your sidekicks tonight?" Skiff asked.

"Home in bed, I guess," Jock said, winking at Bunny. "We were on the way to a show ourselves, but we thought we'd stop by just to make sure you weren't lonely."

Skiff made a funny, snorting noise. "Fat chance, with that dance going on over at the Yacht Club!" He wandered off to talk to one of the fishermen.

Jock put a dime in the record player. His tanned fingers drummed the counter restlessly. Then as Bunny heard another faint rapping, she turned on the stool. Instead of coming in, Blackie had pressed his face against the glass of the small window just beyond them.

Jock rose quickly. "Well, guess we might as well be shoving." There was no sign of Blackie outside. It was not until they reached the parking lot that they saw him sitting on the low concrete wall that held back the lawn of the park. His cigarette made a tiny red rosebud of light in the darkness.

"How'd everything go?" Jock asked.

"Couldn't have been better," Blackie replied.

They got into the convertible with Blackie in the back as before. "We might as well head over to Beasley's right now," Jock said as he started the motor.

"Why go to Beasley's, why can't we stay here?" Bunny asked.

"Blackie has the radio for that high school kid. We promised to deliver it tonight."

Bunny nodded vaguely, not being particularly interested. As they swung out of the parking lot onto the wide avenue leading into town, the convertible leaped forward with a challenging roar. "For gosh sakes, don't try to set any speed records. This is no night to get picked up by a cop," Blackie warned.

"I'm not going fast." Jock sounded annoyed.

Behind them, Blackie had turned to look out the car window. He leaned forward, his face strangely white. "Don't look now, buddy boy, but I think we've got a car tailing us."

"It can't be the cops, I'm only going thirty," Jock protested.

"Remember what happened to Tor, he was only going twenty-five, and they pulled him over and searched him for nothing," Blackie said.

Bunny squirmed around to look back, too. A block behind them she could see headlights, but she couldn't make out the car. "It's probably someone from the Yacht Club dance," she said, "but if you think it's the police, why don't you slow down and let them go by?"

"And give them a chance to wave us over? Don't be crazy," Jock said. "There's one way to find out if they're following us. I'm going to turn right at the next street. You watch and see if they turn, too." The convertible swung to the right at the next corner, shooting down a narrow street lined with darkened warehouses.

As they neared the end of the block and the

street remained deserted, Bunny was about to let out a sigh of relief. Then it froze in her throat. A pair of headlights were turning the corner, and in the bright splash of light of the intersection she saw the telltale black and white of the car.

"It's the cops, all right!" Blackie gasped.

With a squeal of brakes, Bunny was flung against Jock. They were heading back toward the river now on a narrow street that paralleled the avenue. The headlights made the turn, too, only this time there was the wail of a siren and red lights flashed on.

Instead of stopping, Jock made another screeching turn. They hurtled down an alley. Horrified, Bunny stared at him. "Stop! Why don't you stop? We haven't done anything wrong!"

Blackie leaned forward. "Who are you kidding? You expect us to stop with this radio in the car? A little more gas, Jock, you'll shake 'em."

The convertible's speedometer climbed to seventy-five. Bunny sank back against the seat, weak with terror and sickening realization. Of course, the radio was stolen! It was stolen just like the candy bars and cigarettes and that silly yachting cap. She'd really known all along, only she'd closed her eyes. Tom had said the only road ahead for the River Rats was Trouble. Well, she was on that road now, traveling eighty miles an hour with a stolen radio in the car and a screeching police car behind. She closed her eyes and prayed that it would turn into a bad dream. But when she opened them again, they were still racing through the darkness and the police car was gaining.

Blackie leaned forward worriedly. "You're heading for the river."

"It's our only chance to lose them," Jock replied tersely. "You know those little side roads that lead into the park below the marina? If I can get far enough ahead of them on the river road, we'll duck into one of those."

"But they only go into the park a couple hundred yards, then circle out again. If they see us, they'll bottle us up at the other end," Blackie protested.

"We may shake them. If we don't and they block us off, they'll only nab us for speeding. Remember they don't know about the radio. We'll be hidden in the trees long enough to drop it off along with Bunny."

"Smooth thinking." Blackie patted Bunny's shoulder. "Buck up, we're going to get you out of this. And here's Baby." Bunny felt the leatherette case of the portable radio as he shoved it into her arms.

Ahead she saw the silver glint of water through the trees as they sped onto the winding road that followed the river. Jock did not turn into the park at the first entrance. He waited until the police car dropped from sight around a bend, then he swung into the park and cut off his lights, and they jounced down a gravel road in the darkness. Bunny caught another glimpse of silvery river, a picnic table faintly outlined under an oak, before Blackie pushed her out the door. "Wait near the table. We'll be back," he gasped.

As she staggered half-running across the grass, Bunny heard the roar of the car as it turned around and headed back the way they had come.

Silence, sudden and terrifying, closed around her. She made her way to the picnic table and sank weakly onto the bench. The only sounds were the furtive, whispering noises of the wind stirring through the trees, the sly mumble of the river.

Her hand brushed against the radio. She drew it back as though it had been burned. She did not know where Blackie had gotten it. She supposed that the dance going on at the Yacht Club had made a perfect cover for him to take it from someone's car or boat. She set it on the ground. How could she have been such a fool! Tears flooded her eyes.

They vanished and she stiffened. Approaching from the other direction was a glimmer of headlights. It could not be the boys returning this soon. The officers, having failed to cut them off, must be looking for them. Bunny plunged from the table into the darker shadows of the trees. She had been right. A police car came down the road, the beam of its searchlight reaching across the grass.

Her heartbeat became a roaring in her ears as she flattened herself against the trunk of a tree. She closed her eyes. "Please, dear God, oh please help me," she whispered even as some ugly little voice in her conscience whispered that she did not deserve help.

Too late, she remembered the radio that she had left by the picnic table. Apparently, it was partially concealed behind the bench; the searchlight passed over the table without stopping, split into two bright arms on either side of Bunny's tree and moved on. Within seconds, the car was gone again. Bunny let out a choking sob of relief.

She could only guess that the boys had escaped, but she did not know how long it would be before it would be safe for them to return. She did not care. She would not be there. She never wanted to see any of the River Rats again.

Without a backward glance, she left the radio where it sat behind the bench. If the boys did not find it, someone else would. There was no way she could return it to its rightful owner.

Keeping to the shadows, stumbling occasionally over a hummock of uneven grass, she made her way to the edge of the park. As near as she could tell, she was at the southern end, the lights of Skiff's place and the marina hidden by a bend of the river. In her first panic, she had thought of reaching a phone, but she didn't have the money for taxi fare. She couldn't call her mother and scare her needlessly. By veering off a little more to the south, it was only about four miles home. She would walk.

She set off determinedly, crossing the river road and heading down the street beyond. It was no neighborhood for a girl alone at night. The poorly paved street was deserted and filled with murky shadows cast by darkened warehouses. Twice when the headlights of a car came toward her, she squeezed herself into a doorway until it passed. The boys would not understand why she had run away. The police would want to know what she was doing alone in this neighborhood at night.

A short time later, she heard footsteps behind her. As she looked back fearfully, a man in shabby clothes lurched from a doorway and started after her. She walked faster. The trailing footsteps seemed to gather speed, too. Ahead, she saw a service station, but it was closed for the night; so was the row of stores beyond. Panic gathering in her chest, she started to run. She ran until her throat ached and her breath came in gasps. She looked back. The street was empty. Long ago the man must have turned off on some side street.

She regained her breath, feeling young and foolish and sick all over again. Ahead, she saw the welcome lights of the business district. Soon there were people on the sidewalks, passing cars and buses. A laughing couple about her own age came out of a theater. A pinched feeling in her throat, Bunny wondered if she would ever feel like that again—young and happy and free.

How wrong she had been! Taking someone's yachting cap, working the machines for extra candy bars, borrowing boats without the owners' permission—stealing was stealing! Yet she had told herself that as long as she didn't do these things they did not affect her. It was like putting your foot in quicksand, then finding that you couldn't pull it out.

At last she was home and running up the stairs. Her mother, wearing the robe Bunny had given her for Christmas, was watching television. She looked surprised. "Is something wrong? You're home so early."

Bunny glanced beyond her to the clock. It was not possible that it was only ten thirty. Tonight she had lived a lifetime!

"No, Mom, everything's fine. I just thought I'd come home early." She dropped a kiss on her mother's forehead.

As she went down the hall to her bedroom, Bunny prayed that this would be the last lie that she would ever have to tell. Tomorrow she was going to start growing up.

14

Blister Brigade

Bunny had been certain that she would not sleep. Instead, she slept soundly, the sleep of complete exhaustion. When she awoke, shafts of morning sunlight lay across the bedroom floor and her mother was dressing. She slipped hurriedly into a blouse and faded capris and joined her family in the kitchen.

"I suppose you're going to the river today?" Mrs. Taylor questioned coldly.

Staring at her plate, Bunny felt as though she had become a battleground of mixed emotions. One part of her, young and frightened, wanted to blurt out what had happened last night. The other part burned with familiar resentment at her mother's tone of disapproval. "No, I'm not going to the marina. I thought I'd look for a job," she replied.

Mrs. Taylor looked startled. "Bunny, did something happen last night? Would you like to tell me about it?" Her voice was gentler now.

Bunny bit her lip. It wasn't fair the way adults saw through you. "Nothing happened. Can't everyone just leave me alone!" Carrying her dishes to the sink she deposited them with a loud clatter.

"Someone around here's as pleasant as a rattlesnake!" Doug remarked with a whistle.

Bunny stared stonily out the window. Another day she might have smiled at that English sparrow perched on the wires chattering his heart away. This morning his happiness only made her resentful. A fine start she had made on her resolution to turn a new leaf!

She was glad when her mother had gone to work and Doug had taken off for a friend's house, leaving her to sort her confused thoughts. She had made little progress when the phone rang. It was Jock. Bunny stiffened and a strange coldness encased her heart.

"What happened last night? Why didn't you stick around like we told you?" His voice was angry.

"I couldn't," she faltered.

"What do you mean you couldn't?"

"I didn't dare. The cops came and I hid. Then I decided I'd better get out of there. I left the radio."

"Yeah, Blackie and I found it okay." There was a pause. "We had to wait about an hour before we dared come back. I guess you did the smart thing."

Bunny was ashamed of that quiver of relief that swept over her at the note of approval in his voice.

"I'll be around and pick you up in about an hour," he concluded casually.

She felt trapped. "No, don't do that. I can't go."

"What do you mean you can't go? You said you could yesterday." His voice was angry again.

Bunny's eyes flew around the apartment as though somewhere it held an excuse. "My mother is sick," she blurted.

"Lousy break," Jock sympathized. "I'll call you Monday."

Bunny waited until he had hung up. Her hands knotted at her sides. "Liar! Liar!" she shrieked at herself. What was wrong with her? She wanted to break with the River Rats, yet she still feared their disapproval. She supposed it was because they had been her only friends these last months. When they were gone, she would be utterly alone.

She thought of all the little deceptions she had practiced these last months: dreaming that a menial job of wrapping packages was going to take her straight to the top at Paradine's, fooling herself that one year of typing was enough to hold down a secretarial job, pretending to Dan and George that she was older. Now telling another lie to Jock. It wasn't as easy to change one's personality overnight as she had thought.

Hopefully, she made a list. She must break with

the River Rats, improve her relationship with her mother and find a job. At the bottom she wrote "Tom." She was not quite sure why she added his name except that he had said to call if she changed her mind. She followed it with a question mark. There was a limit to the pride that she could swallow in one day.

Accomplishing the first two items on her list was easier than Bunny had expected. She did not tell her mother everything about the River Rats, just that she had realized that they were drifters and was not going to see them again.

"Bunny, I'm so glad," Mrs. Taylor said with such a lilt in her voice that it seemed to lift Bunny's heart right along with it. "As for finding work, I'd call Paradine's and get in touch with the Department of Employment again."

This time, Bunny tried not to be resentful. She told herself that mothers must have been born to give advice.

By Monday morning, she had gathered her courage when Jock called. "I won't be able to come to the river anymore," she told him. "I'm going to look for a job and start working again."

"Are you kidding?" he asked.

"No, I'm not kidding," she replied.

"Man, you turned out to be as square as that dumb Bev," he said. "But suit yourself."

It hurt being called a square. It hurt even more to realize that while she had made the River Rats an important part of her life, the feeling never had been mutual. They would not miss her any more than they had missed Fink or Bev.

Finding a job turned out to be a more difficult problem. When she called Paradine's, she learned that they had tried to reach her, but failing to find her at home they had decided that she was no longer interested. The best they could promise was to keep her in mind. By now there was a long list ahead of her.

Mrs. Pierce at the employment office was equally pessimistic. Soon school would be out and this year's graduates would be seeking jobs. Many of them already had placed their names with the office.

"If you're really serious, I might have something in about two weeks. It's hard work, low pay and seasonal, but the fruit and tomato canneries will be looking for packers," she said.

Cannery work. The last remnant of Bunny's daydreams about being another Mrs. Kearns or Inez DeWitt flew out the window. Then she nodded.

"These next two weeks I'll try very hard to find a job on my own. If I don't, I'll be back for a cannery job."

That was the night she finally called Tom. There was a painful wait while his married sister summoned him to the phone. "This is Bunny Taylor." She tried to make her voice lighthearted. Instead it came out with a funny, croaking sound. "Hear that

187

noise? That's my pride being swallowed. You were right about everything," she admitted.

Tom hadn't forgotten her. "Bunny, this is great!" His voice dropped an octave. "You're all right, aren't you? You aren't in any trouble?"

"No, I'm not in any trouble," Bunny replied. Then, because she had been keeping it bottled up so long without being able to tell anyone, that little croaking noise came back. "Oh, Tom, it was awful! I almost got caught by the police—"

Tom explained that he was on his way to night school, but he would be over to see her as soon as it was out at ten. Bunny could see that her mother did not think much of dates at ten o'clock at night, but when she learned about night school and that Tom would only be staying an hour, she softened a little. At a quarter to ten she even suggested making some cocoa, then withdrew discreetly to her bedroom on the excuse that she wanted to set her hair. Bunny's eyes followed her gratefully.

It was fifteen after ten when she heard Tom's footsteps on the stairs. Except for being a little thinner, he hadn't changed. "You look great," he said with an approving grin. "Here I was expecting to see you all bloody and bowed." Bunny had almost forgotten how wonderful it was to be able to laugh. "Don't let the cover deceive you. Inside I'm a battered mess."

They sat at the kitchen table drinking cocoa while Bunny told Tom about her experiences with the River Rats. "Instead of walking all the way home I wish you had called me to come after you."

Bunny suddenly wished that she had, too. She was learning a lot tonight. No one was so completely independent that he didn't need one good friend to talk to and trust. Tom stirred his cocoa. "I wish I could help you about finding a job. I only know the way that I found mine. It isn't an easy one."

Bunny leaned forward. "I don't care about its being easy."

"The Department of Employment does a great job, but in our age group there are five applicants for each employer. Instead of waiting for them to come looking for me, I decided to go out looking for them. I started at First Street, going into every store and business place on the block, asking if they needed help. When I finished that block I moved on to the next. I figured somewhere there had to be someone who was thinking of putting on help and when I found him, I'd be there first."

"How long did it take you?" Bunny asked.

He grinned. "Six days, fifty blocks and one good pair of shoes. It would be harder for a girl."

"Well, I'll find out tomorrow," Bunny told him.

"A lot of people are going to turn you down," he warned.

Bunny's eyes twinkled. "After selling Dandyware, do you think that's going to throw me?"

The following morning, filled with determination, Bunny started her search at Montgomery's

189

yardage store at the corner of First and Cherry streets. They did not need a clerk. Neither did the paint store next door, Morry's shoe store just beyond, the bookstore, the five and dime or Appel's drugstore. The Valley Finance Company didn't need a file clerk, the bakery didn't need a kitchen helper, the grocery on West Elm didn't even need someone to sweep out. These weren't disembodied voices over a phone turning down housewares. These were real, live people who met her eye to eye, and it was her they were turning down.

"I don't just have blisters on my feet, I have them in my ears, too," Bunny confided to Tom when he called to see how she had gotten along.

The next day was a repetition of the first. The nearest she came to a job was at a small printing office on Sixth Street that hired women occasionally for bindery work. They took down her name in case one of their regular workers didn't show up.

The third day began the same. The market for willing but untrained eighteen-year-old girls was hardly active, Bunny told herself glumly as she left a hardware store. The owner had been particularly unpleasant, it was after one o'clock and she found it hard to tell whether that hollow feeling in her stomach came from disappointment or hunger. By now she had left the center of town and was nearing the waterfront. She could smell the river already, smells that brought back memories of the River Rats and lazy days. Ahead, she saw a second-hand store that looked like a pawnshop and the gray corrugated siding of a small manufacturing concern. It did not look like a fertile field for job hunting, but at the far corner was a restaurant.

The Dew Drop Inn was not as large as it had appeared from up the street, but it was very clean with its counter and half dozen tables surprisingly well patronized for that hour.

Most of the customers seemed to be truck drivers and workers from the nearby warehouse district, but Bunny found an empty seat at the end of the counter. A low partition divided the kitchen area, where a bald, paunchy man of about sixty stood over the stove. A huge, smiling woman of about the same age with dyed, saffron-colored hair, waited on her.

"What'll it be, dearie?" she asked.

"Hamburger and coffee." In spite of that wonderful aroma of home-baked pie, Bunny decided this was all her budget could stand.

The waitress brought Bunny's order and hurried down the counter to where two men were pointing at their empty coffee cups. Apparently, they were customers of long standing. "Sara, your service is getting almost as bad as your coffee," one teased.

"Humph, if the java is so bad why d'ya keep asking for more?" she kidded as she refilled their cups. "As for service—Maggie quit. Maude's got a lame foot and won't be in tonight. If anybody thinks I'm going to move faster than a slow walk when I'm facing a sixteen-hour shift today, he's got another think coming."

The men laughed good-naturedly, but Bunny's face was thoughtful. She'd never thought of working as a waitress. The Dew Drop Inn wasn't any Charmaine's, it wasn't even in a very good part of town. But it was clean, and the woman had said they were short-handed.

Suddenly, her hunger had vanished, and she put down her hamburger. The plump woman was ringing up a sale on the cash register; after that she had to wait on a party at one of the tables and bring some pie for a man at the counter. At last, Bunny caught her eye. "Something wrong with your hamburger, dearie?"

"Oh no, it's very good," Bunny said hurriedly. "I heard you say one of the waitresses had quit. I'm looking for a job."

The woman looked surprised. "You're experienced? Where'd you work last?"

Bunny's heart sank. There was that miserable word *experienced* again. "I've never worked as a waitress, but I know I could learn," she insisted.

The woman's eyes were already getting that veiled look, but she motioned to the man in the kitchen. "Whatsa matter, can't she pay her check?" he asked as he joined them.

The woman shook her head. "She doesn't have any experience, but she wants Maggie's job."

"No experience?" The man started to shake his head.

Suddenly, Bunny was tired of being a zero, of being told all the things she lacked. She had assets, too, and just looking around this place she could see that they could use them. "You can't afford to turn me down," she said. "I may never have worked as a waitress before, but you need me. There are a lot of things I can do."

"Like what?" he asked quizzically.

Bunny smiled. "I can operate a cash register. I am young and strong and don't tire easily. I learn very quickly. I can wash dishes and mop floors. I like people. I get along with strangers—everyone tells me I have a nice disposition—I hardly ever get sick—"

The man held up his hand as if to dam this torrent of virtues. "We only pay thirty dollars a week."

"Plus two meals, uniforms and tips," the woman added.

It didn't sound like much, but Bunny nodded. "That's fine with me."

"The hours are irregular," the man continued. He explained that his wife Sara worked from six in the morning until two, when another woman came on and worked until closing. Bunny would be needed from eleven to eight to help with both lunch and dinner.

"That's all right, too," she agreed.

The couple exchanged looks. "Suppose you could start this afternoon from four to eight to help

193

with the dinner business?" The woman made the decision.

Bunny felt a curious giddiness. "I'll be back at four," she promised. She gave the couple her name and address. In turn, she learned that they were Mr. and Mrs. Peabody, owners of the restaurant.

The man returned to the kitchen, the woman to her job filling coffee cups. Bunny, finding her appetite restored, picked up her hamburger. Mrs. Peabody stopped in front of the pie case. She selected a wedge of chocolate cream and placed it in front of Bunny. "Compliments of the house, dearie. You can call me Sara." She jerked a thumb at her husband. "And he's Sam."

Before she had worked at the Dew Drop Inn a week, Bunny knew that Sam and Sara Peabody were two of the nicest people she had ever met. From the beginning, they had accepted her for exactly what she was, young and inexperienced. Free to be herself, Bunny concentrated on proving her usefulness. She asked questions. In lulls between customers, she voluntarily washed dishes and helped Sam slice vegetables. Because she had always liked people, she made it a game to start learning all the names and preferences of the regular customers. Her reward was the startled appreciation of her employers.

At first, her mother had objected to the job because of the unsavory neighborhood and the fact that Bunny would be coming home after dark. But once she had had Midge drive her past the Dew Drop Inn and had seen its neat interior and learned that Bunny could catch her bus right out in front, she had inexplicably changed her mind, stating it might be good experience.

Physically, the work had turned out to be somewhat harder than Bunny had expected, but her youth had helped her make the adjustment. Friday night, as she waited her turn at the cash register, she even felt a little sorry for Maude Lumberman, the other waitress.

"Oh, my aching feet," Maude complained as she rang up a sale. "To think I paid twenty dollars for a pair of shoes with built-in bunions." A middle-aged woman with frizzy brown hair, Maude had a perpetually gloomy outlook on life.

Tonight, Bunny only had time for a sympathetic nod. Once she had rung up her own sale and given the customers at the first table their change, she moved on to the next table to refill some coffee cups, then hurried back to the counter to serve a truck driver his waiting hamburger and select a piece of pie for a night watchman.

By seven thirty the dinner rush had slacked off. Filling herself a cup of coffee, Maude sat down at the end of the counter with a heartfelt sigh. Bunny continued working, resetting tables, filling creamers and checking napkin holders. For Maude, who remained on duty until ten, this was a last chance to rest. For Bunny, the extra burst of energy came easily now that her day was almost over. At eight o'clock, Maude rose with another sigh and glanced meaningfully at the clock. Bunny did not need to be reminded. She ducked into the small back room, where she emptied her tips into her purse, tossed her apricot uniform into the hamper and changed into her own clothes.

Outside, she waited under the blinking neon sign. There was barely time to wave to Maude, who was watching from the window, before the headlights of the bus bore down on her.

Once she had settled herself on the leather seat, that feeling of weariness vanished. Tonight, her purse held her first paycheck. It had been a long time since she had been able to spend much money on herself. Surely, just one paycheck—she pushed the temptation away.

The bus carried her the seven short blocks into downtown Bolton. Bunny did not transfer immediately to the park bus but hurried up Eighth Avenue. Paradine's had a beautiful display of summer shifts. The store beyond had some adorable baby-doll nightgowns. In the blouse shop was a dusky rose sailor blouse with white piping. Eyes grimly ahead, she continued on to the next corner, where the Merchant's Bank reared its darkened stone façade. Using the cold rump of one of the reclining cement lions for a desk, she endorsed her check and made out a deposit slip. With a feeling of self-righteousness, she shoved the envelope through the metal door of the night drop.

She still had the money from her tips. The

bakeries were closed, but the counter girl at Melton's All-Night Cafeteria obligingly found a paper sack for the three eclairs. Racing down the street, Bunny flagged the nine o'clock bus just as it was pulling away.

Her mother and Doug were still up. "Bunny, I was frantic when you weren't on the eight thirty bus, that's the one you've caught every other night," Mrs. Taylor accused her.

"I'm sorry," Bunny apologized, "but this was pay day."

Her mother's face froze. "Bunny, you didn't buy a lot of gifts?"

Bunny dropped a reassuring kiss on her cheek. "Don't worry, Mom. But it seemed to me we ought to celebrate somehow. I bought three of Melton's eclairs, the ones we all like so well."

Mrs. Taylor's face relaxed. "I think eclairs would be delicious."

Doug looked disappointed. "Golly, you mean I don't get a new game or anything?"

"Indeed you don't!" Bunny told him with mock severity. "And if you don't stop complaining, you won't even get your eclair."

Doug gave her a scowling look, but Bunny noticed that he was already climbing the stepstool to get down the glass plates that they always used for special treats.

"While I was between bus stops, I put my check in the night drop at the bank. I plan to do that every week," Bunny told her mother.

"You mean you banked all of it?" Mrs. Taylor asked. "Bunny, I'm glad that you plan to be more careful with your money, but you don't want to go from one extreme to the other. You'll need some money."

"I still have my tips," Bunny explained.

"How much did they come to?" her mother asked.

Bunny shifted uncomfortably. "I don't know."

"You don't know?" her mother ejaculated. Even Doug, a fringe of whipped cream around his mouth, stopped eating to stare at her.

Bunny's face reddened. "That first night when I only worked four hours, they were almost three dollars. That's when I made up my mind not to count them again. I thought if I waited until the end of the week, they'd come as a big surprise and help me to work harder. I suppose it was childish—"

Her mother's eyes twinkled. "I wouldn't say it was childish, Bunny." She began to chuckle. "It—it just sounds like *you*."

Looking slightly perplexed, Bunny went to the bedroom for the old curler bag into which she had been dropping her tips every night. It felt astonishingly heavy. Except for three one-dollar bills, all was in change, mostly quarters. When she had emptied it onto the kitchen table and counted it, her face was unbelieving. Forty-three dollars! "That's more than my wages! All together it's more than I earned at Paradine's." Bunny divided the money into two equal piles and shoved one across the table.

Her mother shook her head. "No, you save it. Someday, you may decide to go back to school."

Bunny felt that familiar bristle of defiance. "I'm never going back to school."

Instead of the expected protest, her mother merely shrugged. "Save it then, in case you lose your job again."

Bunny shook her head. "I won't lose this one. If the Peabodys had to let someone go tomorrow, it would be Maude. I'm younger and stronger than she is, I work harder and I don't complain. Just yesterday, Mrs. Peabody told me I was helping business." She was not bragging; she was simply being honest.

"I still do not intend to accept money for your room and board. At least not until you're twenty-one," her mother said. Rising, she carried her plate to the sink. "Since you apparently plan to be a waitress all your life, I suggest you still save your money—for the day when you are too old and tired and have aching feet." There was a light, teasing note to her voice, but as Bunny returned the money to her curler bag her face was thoughtful.

15

Where Tomorrow?

Bunny had chosen the Bamboo Palace again, because that was where Tom had taken her to celebrate his getting a job. By marvelous coincidence, they even got the same little booth again— with a moon-shaped pink paper lantern above them and on the wall a drawing of a smoke-breathing dragon who seemed to be swallowing his own tail. But Tom refused to let Bunny make it her treat.

"You went with the wrong crowd too long. None of that 'dutch' stuff for me. When I take a girl out, I do it in style," he insisted.

Bunny thought of the River Rats and their careless attitude toward money. She had called it democratic, when actually it had been nothing but a leveler that reduced them all to a common denominator. "I can remember when you weren't so particular," she teased, recalling their first meeting.

"I was unemployed then. Now I'm a working man; I can afford you."

Bunny smiled. "I still don't feel right about it. Dinner was my suggestion. You only invited me to a show."

"Gold digger," Tom said. "But if you're determined to shower me with your hard-earned money, you can buy me a graduation present."

"A graduation present?" Bunny gasped. "You mean you're finishing school this June?"

"You mean I'm finishing—finally!" he corrected wryly. "There won't be any ceremony, but after my last class they'll put my diploma in the mail."

"That hardly seems fair," Bunny protested. "Bells should ring. You should wear a cap and gown."

His eyebrows tilted quizzically. "Hey, I thought you were the girl who claimed graduation ceremonies weren't important."

Bunny flushed. "It's different when it's you. I mean—you're important."

"I'm glad you feel that way," Tom said soberly; then he grinned. "But if you ever get those mixed-up thoughts of yours straightened out, you might remember that you're important, too."

Bunny dropped her eyes. She supposed she did sound a bit confused, insisting that graduation was important for Tom but not for her.

There was nothing confusing about her work at the Dew Drop Inn. The last of May was hot in Bolton, and the overhead fans had trouble keeping down the heat from the griddle and coffeemakers. As the newness of the job wore off, there were times when Bunny had to admit it had a kind of dreary sameness, but there was a pleasant sense of security in knowing that she finally had found something at which she could excel.

Through her renewed friendship with Tom, Bunny began to realize how lonely independence could be. She thought back over this last year and the varied people who had slipped into and out of her life: some enemies, some friends, some indifferent. Yet all had given her something, if nothing more than a better understanding of human nature that made it easier for her to deal with customers at the café. But she knew now that a hundred new acquaintances could never take the place of a few real friends.

She got in touch with Anna Finch again. Because of their different working hours, there was no way they could get together for either lunch or dinner; but occasionally on her way to work Bunny dropped by the store, and once a week they got together for a good chat on the telephone.

She phoned Pam and Eileen and arranged for all three of them to visit Sandy one Sunday afternoon. Even with her new baby son to keep her busy, Sandy must have missed them, for the apartment was spotless and she had made a fancy dessert. The three of them had gone together to buy a car bed for the baby. On the way over Bunny had kept it secret, but she also had bought two smaller gifts for Pam and Eileen, who would be graduating in two weeks.

The four of them had a wonderful visit. Eileen already had found a job for after graduation, working as a file clerk for a large company. "It only pays forty a week as a trainee, but there's a good chance for advancement," she said.

Pam wasn't looking for a job. She'd won a scholarship to a small college in Oregon and was going to spend her vacation at home sewing the clothes she'd need in the fall. Sandy and Jack were looking around for a small house to rent. Forgetting false pride, Bunny told them about her new job. It might not sound as grand as working at Paradine's but she was making good money.

"Why, I think it sounds wonderful!" Sandy cried. "Imagine working down there in the industrial district where most of your customers are men. You'll land a husband in no time."

Everyone, including Bunny, burst into laughter. Sandy, happily married at seventeen, was determined to be a matchmaker for the rest of them. Bunny realized suddenly that as they grew older, it was only normal that they should begin to develop different interests, but that did not mean that the warm core of friendship still wasn't there.

A week later, she ran into Kay Southern while she was waiting for her bus downtown. Kay looked wonderful, with tanned cheeks and new short hair-cut. As usual she was bubbling with plans. She was graduating from JC that week end, in the fall she was going on to the state university, but she would be returning to Paradine's Campus Shop for the summer. "So we'll be able to have lunch together again," she cried, squeezing Bunny's arm.

There was a funny, tight feeling in Bunny's throat. She remembered that the last time she had seen Kay had been when she had come into the store at Christmas. "I haven't been at Paradine's since February," she said.

Kay's face was stunned. "Oh, I didn't know. I've only been back a couple of times since the holidays. When I didn't see you at the stocking counter I figured you were back in the wrapping department." Her face brightened. "I bet you got tired of wrapping packages and quit to take a better job?"

"No, I got fired," Bunny admitted honestly. "But I have a new job now. I'm a waitress."

If Kay remembered all those grand dreams Bunny had confided over their lunches at Paradine's, she was too polite to say anything. "Why, how nice. I'll drop in during my lunch hours. We'll still see each other."

Bunny shook her head. "That would be nice, but I don't work downtown. It's a small place down on First and Dock streets near the river."

Kay looked crestfallen, then she managed a weak smile. "At least, it's a job." There was no time to say more. Bunny's bus had arrived.

It was too early for the afternoon breeze from the river, and the big circulating fans were having trouble keeping the Dew Drop Inn cool. Sara, red-cheeked and perspiring, had been waiting for Bunny's arrival so that she could get over to the bank. This meant Bunny had to handle the lunch-hour crowd alone. Mr. Wetherly, the security guard at the tool plant, was crotchety and didn't want his usual ham on rye. The three men at the end of the counter required about a gallon in coffee refills. The four girls from the dry cleaning plant took a table today instead of sitting at the counter, which meant extra trips. Sara hadn't fixed enough pats of butter, and they ran out of dill pickles.

By two o'clock, most of the lunch crowd had left, but Bunny was still relieved to see Maude coming through the door.

She took over while Bunny sat down gratefully to eat the tuna salad and cheese sandwich Sam had fixed for her.

"You're the quiet one today," Maude observed.

Bunny swallowed a bite of sandwich. "How long have you been a waitress, Maude?" she asked.

"All my life," Maude said wearily. "Or maybe it just seems that way. If you're really interested, about twenty years—and the last fifteen my feet have been killing me."

Bunny chuckled, because she knew Maude expected it; but as she bit into her sandwich again, her eyes clouded. She wondered suddenly where she would be in twenty years.

Leave it to Kay, frank and discerning, to put things in their proper perspective. "At least, it's a job," she had said. Bunny was contented with her work, she was even making better money than any of her friends, but she realized abruptly that there was one big difference. Kay, Ann, Eileen, Pam, even Sandy, all had a future ahead of them. She had settled for just a job.

She was on a ladder that led nowhere. She was content now but where would she go tomorrow? There was no one ahead of her, no place to advance. There was no reason that she couldn't hold onto this job forever. But where would she be? Another Maude Lumberman with aching feet.

That night, Bunny got off the bus four blocks from the apartment and walked the rest of the way. She could think better when she walked.

Her mother looked up anxiously as she came through the door. "I saw the bus go by five minutes ago. I wondered where you were."

Bunny gave her an affectionate hug. "I got off a couple of blocks early. I wanted to think a little." She hesitated. "Mom, do you still have that Miss Carmichael's telephone number?"

"Bunny! You don't mean it!" Mrs. Taylor cried in happy disbelief.

Bunny tried to cling to a few shreds of pride and independence. "Now mind, I'm not promising anything. I just thought I'd talk to her."

Bunny's appointment was for the following Monday morning, and Mrs. Carmichael turned out to be very understanding. "I'm not coming to see you because I'm out of work. I have a job, and I'm making more money than I was before," Bunny said once she was seated in the counselor's office at the high school.

Miss Carmichael smiled. "For that very reason you're even more welcome. Unemployment alone drives some dropouts back to school; but for a young person, who is making his way successfully, to consider giving up a job to resume his education requires a big decision."

"I'm not sure that I want to give mine up. I was really thinking of night school," Bunny explained.

"Let's take a look at your record and see what you need," Miss Carmichael suggested. Because Bunny had phoned in advance for the appointment, she already had one folder on her desk. Now she left the room to get the rest of her records.

As Bunny waited, the sound of a distant buzzer filled the hall with scuffling footsteps. From the window she saw young people pouring across a green quadrangle of lawn to the auditorium steps. It was the senior class gathering for graduation practice. She caught a glimpse of red hair that could have been Eileen's.

Miss Carmichael's return brought her eyes back into the room. As the counselor looked over Bunny's jumbled record, she frowned.

208

Bunny misunderstood. "I know my grades were pretty bad," she admitted.

Miss Carmichael shook her head. "I wasn't thinking of that. Until the last semester, your grades were quite adequate. No, I was just thinking of how we failed you."

"Failed me?" Bunny was startled.

Miss Carmichael nodded. "I've been a counselor here for three years. Yet in all that time, you never voluntarily came to see me for advice. Because you were not a discipline problem, no one forced you to come. Yet here in your record, in your shifting from one course to another, I see your discontent, your restlessness, the warning that you were heading toward being a dropout. That's one of the things that we learned from our survey. Sometimes we must share the blame for not reaching students with courses that interest them."

Bunny shook her head. "I don't think anyone could have interested me. I still don't know what I want to be."

"We might have helped," Miss Carmichael persisted. Then she smiled broadly. "But the important thing is what we can do *now*."

They talked about adult night school. Even by switching to Northside High School, which was closer downtown, it would be impossible for Bunny to get away from the café in time for the start of the evening classes at eight o'clock. "My employers are very considerate, they might arrange to let me off at seven one or two nights a week," she said helpfully. "How long would it take to get my diploma?"

Miss Carmichael did some figuring. "Two—probably three years."

"Three years? I'd be twenty-one!" Bunny gasped. By then Pam would almost be through college, Eileen would have three years' seniority with her company, Sandy would probably have a home of her own and a couple of children. "Isn't there a quicker way?" she asked.

"For you there is," Miss Carmichael said. "Many dropouts, because of their discipline records or because they've waited until they are too old, aren't eligible to return to regular high school classes. Night school is their only choice. But you've only been out one year. You'd only be a few months older than your classmates. If you want to return this fall, I think I can get you reinstated as a regular student at South Bolton High. A year from now you would graduate with our present junior class."

Bunny's eyes drifted toward those young people on the auditorium steps. That was her class being graduated this year. All her friends were being graduated now!

"It would be losing a year out of my life, like tearing up this last year and throwing it away," she cried.

"Experience is never lost," Miss Carmichael reminded. "You've learned things this last year that will be valuable all your life, things you would

210

never learn in school. This year has given you a new maturity, a maturity you might even share with some of your classmates next year by becoming an active school leader instead of just a passive hanger-on."

Bunny hesitated. She knew without Miss Carmichael's telling her that in another year she would not be able to make this offer again. By then Bunny would be too old. It had to be this fall or never. It wouldn't be easy. All her closest friends would be gone. It would be hard getting back into study habits again. She'd feel so much older than everyone else. There were a thousand excuses, yet deep in her heart she already knew her answer. "I'll come back," she agreed.

Miss Carmichael arranged for her to return for an aptitude test that would help her in choosing her course. As Bunny went down the wide front steps, she remembered that last time she had raced down them, almost a year ago. She avoided looking toward the young people practicing outside the auditorium. Except for one foolish, headstrong decision, she might be with them today.

"If we keep coming here, we should own the place before long," Tom said.

Bunny poked at a piece of water chestnut and smiled at him across the black and red lacquered table at the Bamboo Palace. "Didn't you know, that's what my aptitude test recommended?"

"That you buy a Chinese restaurant?" Tom teased.

"Silly! That I would be good as a restaurant hostess, a receptionist or interviewer, anywhere that I can work with people."

Bunny told him about the course Miss Carmichael had helped her select. Senior English and world problems to fulfill her college prep requirements so that she would be able to get into junior college if she should decide to continue her education. Second-year typing and business math, in case she didn't want to go on and to utilize the year of each that she already had taken. And finally, psychology, because of the findings of the aptitude test and the hope it might pique her interest. It would mean hard work, but it was a course tailored to fit her individual needs.

Tom seemed very impressed. He was equally impressed with the electric shaver she gave him as a graduation present. "You shouldn't have spent that much money, though," he told her sternly.

Bunny thought of Pam and Eileen, who had been graduated two nights ago with caps and gowns and a big all-night party. In contrast, her gift and a simple dinner at the Bamboo Palace seemed a rather modest celebration. Keeping her voice light, she twisted her face into what she hoped was a wicked leer. "What makes you think I paid for it? Remember, I have some light-fingered buddies down by the waterfront."

Tom, who knew the memory of the River Rats still gave her nightmares, burst into laughter. "You can't sell me that story," he insisted.

212

Bunny pouted and shrugged. "Okay, if you insist on the truth. The only reason I gave you such a lavish gift is that I was thinking of next year when I'll be graduating."

"That sounds more like it," Tom agreed with a twinkle in his dark eyes. "I'll try to remember you with some little geegaw."

"Preferably mink or emeralds," Bunny added airily.

"Any objection to diamonds?" Tom asked. "Being an educated man, I couldn't possibly propose to any girl without a high school diploma, but after next June I might be able to put you on my serious list."

He was teasing, but behind that grin there was something warm and gentle in his eyes. Bunny busied herself with another piece of water chestnut. It was rather pleasant thinking of being on Tom's serious list. But there was one lesson she had learned. It couldn't be rushed and it couldn't be held back—Tomorrow would get here in its own sweet time.

29501 COUNT ME GONE, by Annabel and Edgar Johnson. A rebel and misfit at eighteen, Rion rejects the values of "the other generation" and searches for his own answers to what he is going to do with his life. (75¢)

29513 JUST MORGAN, by Susan Beth Pfeffer. Morgan begins a different, independent life when she becomes the ward of her sophisticated uncle, a famous writer living in New York City. (75¢)

29504 CHILDREN OF THE RESISTANCE, by Lore Cowan. Eight dramatic, true stories of teenagers who fought for freedom in the underground resistance movement in Europe during World War II. (75¢)

29277 ACROSS THE TRACKS, by Bob and Jan Young. Betty Ochoa, third generation Mexican-American, finds a new pride in her heritage as she helps to achieve better understanding between the Mexican and "Anglo" students in her California high school. (60¢)

29251 HOLD FAST TO YOUR DREAMS, by Catherine Blanton. Determined to overcome all obstacles—even a direct attack because her skin is brown—fifteen-year-old Emmy Lou courageously struggles to win the laurels of a ballet star. (60¢)

29508 "NATIONAL VELVET," by Enid Bagnold. When Velvet Brown won a piebald in a village raffle, she began a glorious adventure that would take her all the way to the Grand National, the greatest race in the world. (75¢)

29574 JUNIOR MISS, by Sally Benson. The heartwarming and hilarious adventures of the one and only Judy Graves as she tackles the joys and heartaches of growing up. (75¢)

29534 HELTER-SKELTER, by Patricia Moyes. Felicity—better known as "Cat"—looked forward to two weeks of nothing but fun and sailing, until a strange, unsolved mystery led her on a dangerous quest for a murderer. (75¢)

29299 THE DEVIL'S SHADOW: *The Story of Witchcraft in Massachusetts,* by Clifford Lindsey Alderman. The terrifying drama of the witch trials in Salem in 1692—and how the madness started with the accusations of a small group of girls. (60¢)

29295 HAUNTED SUMMER, by Hope Dahle Jordan. When the newspaper headlines screamed *Hit and Run Driver,* Rilla became a hunted and haunted person as she desperately tried to hide the secret of her involvement in the accident. (60¢)

29289 LIGHT A SINGLE CANDLE, by Beverly Butler. When Cathy lost her sight at the age of fourteen, she had to abandon her dreams of being an artist. But with the help of a guide dog, a new life of independence and promise opens up for her. (60¢)

29507 WHERE DOES THE SUMMER GO? by Ethel Edison Gordon. This was to be a very special summer for Freddy as her relationship with David deepened into a disturbing but intensely exciting experience. (75¢)

29315 THE STORY OF PHILLIS WHEATLEY: *Poetess of the American Revolution,* by Shirley Graham. The moving story of the brilliant, young Afro-American whose poetry won her recognition in America and England and praise from Tom Paine and General George Washington. (60¢)

(If your bookseller does not have the titles you want, you may order them by sending the retail price, plus 25¢ for postage and handling to: Mail Service Department, POCKET BOOKS, a division of Simon & Schuster, Inc., 1 West 39th Street, New York, N. Y. 10018. Please enclose check or money order—do not send cash.)